strange dreams

WELCOME TO CAMBIO SPRINGS.

In the desert town of Cambio Springs, the water is cool, the summers sizzle, and all the residents wear fur, feathers, or snakeskin on full moon nights. In a world of cookie-cutter shifter romance, head to the desert for something different.

In "Long Ride Home," Jena Crowe escaped the Springs ten years ago. Now, she's heading home with two boys to start a new life. With her husband's ghost keeping her company on the road, Jena will learn that moving back and moving backward aren't necessarily the same thing, and sometimes the places you try to escape are exactly where you need to fall.

In "Five Mornings," Alex McCann and Teodora 'Ted' Vasquez never had a simple relationship... but you couldn't call it a boring one either. Five mornings in their past shape who they will become to each other. To their families. And to the mysterious town they call home.

In *Stings & Arrows*, Sean Quinn escaped Cambio

Springs with nothing but the clothes on his back, fleeing from a scorned clan, an unearned reputation, and the weight of family history. Wandering the world as a travel photographer suited him, until he met one fellow wanderer who would upset everything he thought about his future.

Strange Dreams is an anthology of two previously published short stories, "Long Ride Home" and "Five Mornings," with an all new prequel novella, *Slings and Arrows*, by ten-time USA Today bestseller, Elizabeth Hunter, author of the Cambio Springs series and the Elemental Mysteries.

strange dreams

Tall Tales from Cambio Springs

Elizabeth Hunter

recurve press, llc

Strange Dreams
Copyright © 2023
Elizabeth Hunter
ISBN: 978-1-959590-20-0

long ride home

Jena Crowe escaped the Springs ten years ago. Now, she's heading home with two boys to start a new life. With her husband's ghost keeping her company on the road, Jena will learn that moving back and moving backward aren't necessarily the same thing, and sometimes the places you try to escape are exactly where you need to fall.

Three nights to say goodbye. Three days to come to grips with the future. For Jena and her two sons, it's going to be a long ride home.

one
night one

Oregon Coast

JENA CROWE MCCANN was driving down the Oregon coast and breathing in the cool night air when her husband's ghost appeared to her. She slid her hand along the car door, pressing down the button that would crack the window open so the smell of pine and salt filled the air. Then she took a deep breath, holding the fragrance in her lungs for as long as she could before she let out a long sigh.

Lowell's ghost kept her company, silently watching the oncoming lights and occasionally glancing over a phantom shoulder at his sons. The boys were sleeping in the backseat, both exhausted after a final day of packing and saying goodbye to friends and the suffocating helpfulness of their neighbors. Lowell's ashes rested in a simple urn carved from cedar and placed into a box with a few other mementos from his too-short life. Jena would give the box to his parents when she and the boys got home.

Home.

"I'm going to miss that smell," Lowell said.

Jena glanced over. "Can you smell that? Really?"

His shadowy outline frowned. "I'm not sure if I can smell it or I just remember the smell of it."

"Well, that clears everything up."

"Hey, I'm as new at this being a ghost business as you are at seeing ghosts."

"I don't see ghosts. I just see you."

"Really? Never before?"

"Don't you think I would have told you if I saw ghosts?"

Lowell smiled and leaned back in the seat, turning his head so he stared at her profile in the low light from the dashboard. "I don't know. You always had your secrets."

"I didn't keep secrets from you."

"I didn't say you *kept* them from me, just that you had them. It's okay. I like that I never figured you out completely. You were my favorite puzzle."

A sharp ache pierced her heart. "Am I still going to see you when we get there?"

"I don't know."

She drove on in silence, his soft voice keeping her company on the twisting roads lined by dark conifers.

"Do you think I'm making a mistake?" Jena asked. "Moving so soon?"

"No. It's a good move. It'll be a new start for all of you."

"I feel like I'm moving backward."

"Nah." He grinned. "Moving back, not backward."

"What's the difference?"

"You know. You're just not seeing it." He crossed his

arms. Arms that had once held her tightly. Held their sons. Thrown darts at their favorite pub in college. Arms that had carried her name. The boys' names. Favorite verses and patterns tattooed permanently onto all too un-permanent skin.

"I miss your arms, Low."

"I miss your everything."

She blinked back tears and forced herself to focus on the road. In the rearview mirror, she saw her youngest, Aaron, shift in his seat. Lowell turned his head to stare at the small boy who was the spitting image of himself.

"The boys need this, Jena. They need to be around family. Even my crazy people."

"Don't forget mine."

"Them too. And our friends. And Joe and Allie's kids. Ted and Ollie and everyone. They need to be in a place where they're going to be understood. Where they won't have to hide."

"I'm afraid for them."

He frowned. "Because of me? That's not how it works; you know that."

"Still, I worry."

"You're a mom. It's part of your job."

She sniffed. "Damn straight it is."

Lowell grinned again. "That's my girl. You'll watch them like a hawk."

"Haha."

He took a deep breath, letting it out slowly as he stared straight ahead. "It's the right move. The boys need to go to your mom and dad's diner every day after school for a milkshake and help with their homework. They need to go fishing with my dad or pull weeds with my mom at the park while being lectured about native plant species and water conservation. They need all that stuff. And you do, too."

"I'm pretty well educated about water conservation already, thanks."

He laughed. "You know what I mean."

"I do." She swallowed the lump in her throat. "I'm going to end up working the grill at Dad's diner."

"You'll class up the place."

"It's not exactly why I went to culinary school."

"I don't know." He settled back, turning his eyes toward the dark road ahead. "You liked Cartwright well enough. It's as small as the Springs."

"Nothing's as small as the Springs. And Cartwright was a college town. It may have been small, but there were plenty of food snobs with disposable incomes to experiment on."

He shifted again, and Jena had to pinch herself. There was no sound when he moved, except the expected whistle of the night wind at the window and the soft snoring of eight-year-old Low Jr. in the backseat.

"Well, now you'll have truckers, farmers, and desert eccentrics to experiment on. The town could use a little shake-up. You're just the woman to bring it. Your dad won't bat an eye when you add duck confit hash to the breakfast menu. It'll go great with a side of your mom's gravy."

Jena winced. "That's wrong on so many levels. I'm not even going to respond."

Lowell laughed, the rich, welcome sound echoing in the tightly packed car. He looked over his shoulder at the sleeping boys. He watched them silently for a few moments, then looked around the car before his green eyes settled on Jena.

"I'm glad we spent the money on the Subaru. You'll like the all-wheel drive out in the desert. This thing will last a long time. Really safe, too."

Jena looked over to meet his eyes when the road straightened out. A smile lingered on his lips, and blond hair fell over his forehead. He looked the same. He looked better. Like he had when he was a vibrant young man before the cancer had ravaged his body and stolen the light from his eyes.

"Mom?"

Jena blinked away her tears, and he was gone. She looked into the rearview mirror at her five-year-old son. "What's up?"

Aaron yawned, his round cheeks stretching as his arms reached out, whacking his older brother, who grunted and shifted away.

"I need to go potty. When do we get there?"

"Not for a while, Bear. We'll stop for a break, okay?"

"Okay."

Jena stared at the urn in the passenger seat for a moment before she turned her eyes back to the road and kept driving.

two
day one

Northern California

OUT OF THE corner of her eye, Jena saw Aaron blow hot breath on the window before his small finger squeaked out the figure of a tree that matched the towering pines that soared along the side of the road.

"Mom, will there be trees there?"

Low said, "Stupid, you've been there before. We're just moving to Grandpa and Grandma Crowe's house."

"Mom! He called me—"

"Low, don't call your brother stupid. And yes, there are trees, but not this many."

"Mostly weird Joshua trees," Low mumbled. "They're not really trees. Not real ones. I told you, Aaron. It's the same place we go every Christmas."

Aaron's small forehead wrinkled. "But we didn't live there, then."

Low sighed, and his voice softened. "Bear, a place

doesn't change just because you're moving there instead of visiting."

"Well, I didn't know that. I've never moved before."

"Yeah, you have. We moved four years ago."

Jena glanced up. "You remember that, Low? You were only four."

Her oldest son slumped down. "No." He looked out the window. "Dad told me about it."

Jena didn't say anything. She and Lowell had planned the move back to their childhood home as soon as he was diagnosed, resigned that they hadn't managed to outrun the peculiar curse that had kept them away for so long. If he'd lasted longer, Lowell would have joined them, but the cancer that attacked his brain had shown no mercy. Her husband was gone within five months.

"If you were four, then how old was I?" Aaron asked.

"One." Jena smiled. "And you wanted to get down and walk everywhere. We put your portable crib up in the living room, and you chattered to every one of our friends who were helping us move."

"But you liked it, right, Mom?"

She smiled. "Yep. You were telling me stories even then; I just didn't understand 'em."

Aaron grinned. "What did you do, Low?"

Low was still staring out the window sullenly, so Jena answered. "He mostly hung out with Daddy and Grandpa Max."

Thick as thieves. Despite their different temperaments, her oldest son and her husband had been inseparable. She saw Low blinking hard and tried to distract him. "Hey,

Low, Grandpa Max says he has a fishing trip all planned out for next weekend."

Aaron piped up. "Can I go, too?"

"I think so."

Low finally spoke. "I don't know. It might be a real fishing trip. Not one for babies."

"Mom! Low called me a—"

"Don't call your brother a baby, Lowell."

The boy muttered, "Don't call me Lowell, *Jena*."

A red haze fell over her eyes, and Jena swung the car to the curb with a jerk. Thank God they were on a wide stretch of road. She shut off the car and got out, walking around to pull open her son's door. She could already see the embarrassed tears in Low's eyes as he unbuckled his seatbelt. Aaron stared at them both, open-mouthed.

She slammed the door after he stepped out, marched him to the back of the car, beyond the sight of his younger brother, then spun on him.

"Not in a million years, Lowell McCann! Not in a million years do you talk to me that way. Do you understand?"

He blinked hard, and the tears rolled down his red cheeks. "Yes, ma'am," he whispered.

"What do you think your father would say if he heard you?"

"He'd be mad."

"You bet he would." Jena was blinking away her own tears as she stood in front of her son with her hands on her hips. His shoulders were slumped, and he was sniffing and wiping his nose with the sleeve of his T-shirt. In a second,

Jena swept him into her arms and held him tight. She could feel Low's tears soaking her collar as she bent down to his ear.

"Aaron doesn't understand any of this, buddy. And I know there's a lot that you don't understand either. Hell— don't use that word—there's a lot *I* don't understand, but I know this is the right thing. And it's what your dad wanted. I know you miss your friends and—"

"It's not about my friends," he mumbled.

Jena stroked his thick brown hair, so like her own. "I know it's not. But you're giving up a lot more in this move than Aaron is. I know that."

"Why did he want us to move, Mom? He loved it in Oregon."

"I know." She paused and watched the Subaru rock as a truck drove past, then peeked inside to see Aaron craning his neck to watch them. "He did, but he loved us more. And he knew...." *Oh, Lowell, what did you think you knew? Why were you so adamant about going back to a place we tried so hard to leave?*

Low was still looking at her like a lost child. Jena said, "Your dad knew the Springs were going to be the best place for us. That we needed to be there, I guess."

"But why?"

So many reasons. But she said, "For family. You'll find out when we get there. And as much as I'm not looking forward to it, I think Dad was right. I think we need to go back. Otherwise, we wouldn't be doing this."

They stood in silence, Jena's arms still wrapped around her tall boy. Low finally said, "I'm sorry, Mom."

"I know."

"You only called Dad 'Lowell.'"

"That's not completely true. I call you 'Lowell' when I'm really mad at you."

He sniffed again. "Are you still mad?"

"You ever going to call me Jena again?"

"Only if we're at the grocery store, and you're not answering to 'Mom.'"

"Promise?"

"Promise."

She ruffled his hair and walked him back to his side of the car, reaching into the front seat to grab a bunch of Kleenex. She handed a few to Low, then blew her own nose, closing her eyes as she sent up a silent plea. *Oh, Lowell, I hope you know what you're doing.* By the time she walked back to the driver's seat, Aaron and Low were talking again.

"—but there are trees, right?"

"There's not a lot, but there's a few. And there's more by the Springs and the river where Grandpa will take us fishing. Not just Joshua trees. But Joshua trees are really kind of cool." Low glanced at Jena as she started the car. "They look like some of those weird trees in Dr. Seuss books."

"Cool! Can we have one in our yard?" Aaron asked.

"You mean Grandpa and Grandma's yard?"

Jena said, "Hey, we're going to have our own yard eventually."

"Mom, can we have a Joshua tree for a Christmas tree?"

Low snorted. "Goof, you can't use a Joshua tree for Christmas."

"Mom! Low called me a—"

"Aaron, let it go."

She heard Low cackle from the backseat as Aaron huffed and slumped down below her line of vision in the rearview mirror.

It was going to be a long ride home.

three
night two

Central California Coast

"YOU KNEW GOING into this that I wasn't a good long-term prospect, Jena."

"You're an awful big smart-ass for a ghost."

"You always had a weakness for smart-asses." Low grinned again. At that moment, he was the boy who threw toads at her while she was in her Easter dress. The awkward twelve-year-old who was shorter than her and pissed off about it. The rangy high school boy who gave Jena her first kiss. The boy she married at eighteen, crazy in love and knowing in her heart that she didn't have long.

His grin turned into a soft smile, and ghostly fingers trailed down her cheek. "We had long enough."

"No, we didn't."

He glanced over his shoulder at the sunburned, sandy boys who had played hard on the beach in Monterey after a visit to the aquarium. They would stop the next morning at a college friend's house in Santa Barbara. Jena still felt like driving at night with the window cracked open to the night air. That night, the scent of cedar and eucalyptus filled the salty ocean air as they drove along Highway One. She was tired, but if she drove at night, she knew Lowell would keep her company. Once again, in her heart, she knew she didn't have long.

"You know, if we'd had longer," he said, "I probably would have knocked you up at least twice more. We have very cool kids."

She managed a smile. "We do. They're loud and obnoxious and brilliant."

"And completely ours."

She glanced at him, noticing the look of quiet awe. He'd always watched the boys that way when they slept like he couldn't quite imagine that they existed. In a way, it was extraordinary they did.

"We had longer than most," she whispered.

"Yeah."

She tried to lighten the heavy atmosphere in the car before she choked up. "And really, the fact that you survived until adulthood is a miracle in itself, considering how clumsy you were."

He scowled. "I wasn't clumsy."

"Treehouse. That's all I'm gonna say."

"That was not an accident! I... pushed you."

Jena threw her head back and laughed. "Only you would try to cover up clumsiness as aggression! You didn't have a mean bone in your body, Lowell McCann, and you would *never* have pushed a girl out of a tree house on purpose. *Clumsy*."

"I was devious." He nodded, and his lower lip stuck out

thoughtfully. "I was so devious that I made everyone think I was a nice kid."

"You *were* a nice kid. Just a clumsy one."

"I wasn't! I was the best forward on the basketball team."

Jena rolled her eyes. "Low, there were fifty boys in our entire class."

"That doesn't negate my contribution. And *you* didn't even make the team, despite being the tallest girl in class."

She shrugged. "I don't like basketball."

"The one thing I was good at, and you were completely unimpressed."

She smiled then and looked at him. "You were good at a lot of stuff."

Lowell knit his hands behind his head and leaned back with a grin. "Tell me. All the stuff I was good at. I missed the funeral."

"Cocky." She paused, but he didn't say another word, so she continued in a quiet voice. "You were funny. You could make anyone laugh. And kind. It's like... even though you caused all sorts of trouble, you couldn't stand to see a girl cry. Remember when we were all freshmen, and Allie was still kind of chubby?"

"Yeah."

"And Joe and Alex were picking on her."

"Joe was an idiot. She was in love with him even back then."

Jena nodded. "She was. And you knew it. And they were picking on her that one day after the band concert, and you were there—"

"I didn't say anything mean to her! She was your best friend."

"I know." She reached over and put her hand on the center console like she used to when he was still living. She felt a prickling sensation, almost like static electricity, as his ghostly hand covered hers. "No, you did something stupid to Alex. I can't remember…"

"I think I gave him a wedgie."

She burst out laughing. "You did! That's what it was. And he got so pissed, he turned and chased you behind the gym."

Lowell snorted. "I got a bloody nose for that. Alex was always such a tight-ass. I was hoping the wedgie would help."

"But…" Jena smiled again. "They stopped teasing Allie, didn't they?"

He winked at her. "You were never going to kiss me if my buddies kept teasing your best friend. See?" He tapped his temple. "Devious."

"Softie."

"Shhh." A finger ghosted over her lips. "Don't tell anyone."

Jena blinked back her sudden tears and continued. "And you were so smart, even though you got horrible grades."

"School was boring. What else was I good at?"

"You never exaggerated. You always told the exact truth."

His eyebrows furrowed together. "You liked that? I always thought that pissed you off because I'd tell you if your clothes didn't look good."

She squinted. "Well, that part was a little annoying, but otherwise, I liked it."

"Damn, I was a catch, Jen. Despite my inevitably short life span, you were a lucky woman."

She stifled a smile. "Did I tell you how much I loved your modesty? You were always so humble."

"Exceptionally humble. Incredibly modest. A saint, really."

A low chuckle built in her chest. She muffled it, frightened to wake the boys. She turned onto a wider stretch of the twisting road and turned her head to glance over her shoulder. They were both still sleeping.

"I was good at loving you," Lowell said quietly. "I was always good at that."

It was no good. No matter how hard she blinked, Jena was going to cry.

"No..." His silent body scooted closer, and his fingers tried to wipe away the tears. "Don't cry, baby. You're gonna crash, Jena. Slow down. Don't cry."

A quiet sob wrenched from her throat. "I don't know how to do this without you, Low. Dammit, dammit, dammit!" She quickly blinked away the tears, lifting a hand to brush at her cheeks. "I don't know how to do this."

"That's why you're moving back. Because that's where people know how to help. It won't just be you anymore. So it's okay if you don't know. It's okay."

He continued whispering soothing words to her. Sweet endearments and private jokes they'd shared through ten years of marriage. Three years of dating. A lifetime of growing up in the same small town. When she was calm,

Lowell leaned back on his side of the car, staring at her with an uncharacteristically serious expression.

"I want you to fall in love again."

"Ha!" She uttered a quick, bitter laugh. "Right."

"You will. You'll find love again. You're a very loving person. And you deserve it."

"Maybe I don't want to fall in love again. I loved you my whole life."

He grinned. "Not when I pushed you out of the tree-house, you didn't."

"It was an accident."

His voice was a teasing sing-song. "So you say."

"Mo-om," Low Jr. whined from the back seat, mumbling in his sleep. "Tell Dad he's being too loud."

When her shocked eyes dropped from the rearview mirror, Lowell's ghost was gone.

four
day two

Southern California Coast

"MAMA! WATCH ME!"

Aaron jumped up in the waves, bounding up over them as they rolled into the shore. Jena sat on the warm rocks and dug her toes into the sand. Nearby, Low listened to his music, staring out over the glistening water. They both watched Aaron jump in the shallow waves, Jena poised to leap in the moment he wandered too far.

"There aren't any beaches by the Springs. He'll hate that."

Jena turned to look at Low as he spoke. He'd pulled one of his earbuds out, and the faint sound of music whistled to her ears as the wind blew it toward her. "Yeah, that'll be hard for him. I've never seen a kid like water as much as Bear does. But there's the river. And there are beaches on the river where it twists around and forms these nice little inlets. Grandpa Max can teach both of you how to drive the boat. You'll be river rats in no time."

A spark of interest lit the eight-year-old's eyes. "Really? I can drive it?"

Jena shrugged. "As long as it's okay with him. I mean, don't let the sheriff catch you or anything, but Grandpa will teach you. I learned how to drive a boat around your age."

"How far away is the river from the Springs?"

"Just thirty miles or so."

Low didn't say anything. He just stared out at his younger brother again and put the other earbud back in his ear. Soon, the only sound that drifted to Jena's ears on the deserted stretch of beach was the sound of passing cars on the road behind them, the waves, and her youngest son's shrieks of joy.

"MAMA?"

"What's up, baby?"

She closed her eyes in a long blink, drifting as she sat in the sand and the Southern California sun shone on her. The air was damp and cool in the spring breeze, and Aaron tired out from the water and full of his picnic lunch, lay stretched out on his towel with his head resting against her stomach. Low was walking near the tide pools on the edge of the water, poking at the anemones with a long stick of driftwood.

"Did you ever live in a really big city?"

"Like Los Angeles?" Aaron had been fascinated with the idea of driving through the city with its miles and miles of buildings and houses all stuck together. It was more than his five-year-old brain could fathom.

"Yeah."

"Well, after we left the Springs, Daddy and I lived in Seattle. That's not as big as L.A., but it's pretty big."

"Why?"

"Why did we live there?" She ruffled his hair and watched Low pick up a piece of wet kelp and lift it so it flew in the wind. "That's where Mommy went to school to learn how to cook, and Daddy worked there."

"What did Daddy do in the city?"

She smiled at the memories. "He went to school for a little bit, too, but he didn't like it, so he sold cars."

"Cars?" He squinted his green eyes and looked up at her. Aaron was the spitting image of Lowell, from the sandy blond hair that would darken as the years passed—hopefully for many more years than his father—to the pale, freckled skin. He was a McCann through and through. The stubborn Scots-Irish heritage showed not a hint of the Native American blood mixed in her own family tree. Low Jr. looked more like her, sharing her smooth olive skin, dark brown hair with hints of russet, and cheekbones that were the envy of her girlfriends. But both boys had those eyes, Lowell's beautiful green eyes.

"Yep, Daddy sold cars."

"But he didn't sell cars at home. He sold houses."

"Daddy could sell anything to anyone. That's just the way he was."

Aaron sighed and curled into her side. "That's because everyone liked him, huh?"

She blinked back the tears as the wind caught her eyes. "Yep," she whispered. "Everyone loved Daddy."

They sat in silence for a few more minutes. Low had

thrown the kelp out into the ocean and picked up another piece of driftwood. He drew something in the wet sand with one piece, stood back to look at it for a moment, then took the other piece of wood and violently scratched it out. He repeated the action over and over as he walked farther down the beach until a trail of broken marks followed behind him.

"Mommy?"

"What's up, Aar-Bear?"

"Why is Low mad at me?"

Jena pulled her baby up and set him in her lap, his long legs sticking out awkwardly as she tried to hold him. She lay her cheek on the small boy's soft hair and watched as Low hurled both sticks into the ocean, watching as they splashed in the waves. Then he stood, shoulders slumped, staring out over the murky water as an afternoon fog began to roll in.

"He's not really mad at you. He just misses home."

Aaron's spindly arms reached around her, and his fingers played with the feathers of hair behind her ear. Jena smiled. Her youngest had always twisted her hair when he needed comfort, even as a baby.

"And Daddy. I think Low misses Daddy."

She blinked back tears and hugged him tighter. "I think you're right, Bear. He misses Dad."

Aaron's whisper was almost lost in the wind. "I miss Daddy, too."

Jena couldn't speak as she swallowed the lump in her throat. Finally, she said, "We all do."

HOURS LATER, both boys were packed into the car as she drove through the tall buildings of downtown Los Angeles. She could have bypassed the traffic and taken the route through the foothills, but she was in no hurry and didn't want to spoil the excitement for Aaron. Low sat in the back, patiently looking at everything Aaron pointed out in delight and astonishment. The skyscrapers. The Hollywood sign. Mile after mile of houses quickly became repetitive, even to her youngest son.

As Jena turned east, she realized that they were finally pointed in the direction that would take them back to Cambio Springs, the town she had grown up in. The town she had fled with Lowell, desperate fugitives of a fate they thought they could outrun. The town that would shelter her sons as they grew.

"Hey, Mama?"

"Yeah, Bear?"

"Is it much farther?"

She glanced at the sun as it set in her rearview mirror. "Not long now. Go to sleep, Aaron. When you wake up, we'll be home."

five
night three

Mojave Desert

THIS TIME, when Jena cracked her window open to let in the night air, she was hit by the scent of creosote bushes that had just taken rain. The distinctive smell filled the car as she drove down the deserted highway. They had passed the lights of the city, and the stars shone overhead as a full moon hung in the desert sky. Jena noticed that her foot had pressed down on the accelerator as she took deep breaths of the damp creosote.

"You always loved that smell." Lowell watched her with sad eyes as the desert whipped past.

She shrugged. "It's nice enough."

"You loved it. You *love* it."

Jena whispered, "I do."

"Just because I didn't like it doesn't mean that you shouldn't."

"Low—"

"It's okay to be excited, Jen." He smiled, even as his voice grew hoarse. "You're excited to be back. I can tell."

She shook her head. "It's just some kind of instinct. You know that."

"It's part of you. It's a good part of you." He glanced over his shoulder where the boys snored quietly, slumped together as Aaron lay under his older brother's arm. "It'll be a part of them, too."

Jena could feel the tears start to well in her eyes. "Are you sure?"

He ignored her, staring at the boys before he looked back at her. "Hey, baby, want to know a secret?"

She nodded with a jerk as the tears gathered. "Yeah. Sure. What's the secret? God give you the mysteries of the universe while I was driving today? Winning Lotto numbers? The recipe for Grandma Crowe's pie crust?"

He chuckled low in his throat, and Jena sensed him draw nearer. Her skin prickled in awareness, and she could have sworn that, just for a moment, she could feel his warm breath blow across her cheek.

"The secret is..." His voice dropped even lower until he was whispering into her ear. "I was only borrowing you for a little while."

The sob ripped from her throat just as she passed over the last rise before the lights of the Springs glittered in the distance. A sign on the side of the road read, "Cambio Springs Turnoff: 5 miles." Jena pulled the car over to the side of the road, put it in park, and pushed the door open, stumbling into the night. Lowell's ghost met her outside, leaning his ever-more-hazy body against the side of the car.

"Enough!" She shook her head and dashed the tears

from her eyes. "That's it. I'm not going any farther. Get back in the car, Low."

"Calm down, Jena. You need to keep driving."

She paced the side of the road, her feet stirring up red dust as the creosote filled the air. "No."

"Yes."

"No!" she yelled. "You—you were not *borrowing* me! I was yours. We belonged together. We were supposed to beat it. Why did you let go?"

He moved toward her with his hands raised. "We did belong together. For as long as we had. But it's time—"

"It was *not* time!" Her sobs were carried away in the desert wind as she pulled at her hair in frustration. "You're going to disappear as soon as I drive into that town, so I'm turning around. I'm going home!" She walked back to the car, reaching to pull open the door and get in, but suddenly his hand stopped her.

Jena gasped and looked down at the hand that had been her husband's. Her breath caught. It was as clear and substantial as the day he first held it when they were ten years old. Solid. Strong. When she stopped, Lowell lifted his hand and brushed across her damp cheek in one last caress.

"You're almost home." Whatever energy had animated his spirit seemed to drain as she faced him. Jena could see the star-lit night shining through his sandy hair.

"Low..."

"That"— he pointed toward the lights— "is your home. Always has been. I was borrowing you for a little bit, but this has always been your home."

She whispered, "It was *our* home."

"No." He shook his head. "You were my home. The

only home I needed to live for as long as I could. But you..." She saw him swallow hard. "You need more. You need this place."

She shook her head as he continued. "It's okay to go back. It's okay to be glad. To be relieved. You've been hiding for so long, but now..." He sighed, and the wind blew, making the outline of him waver before her eyes. "You'll drink from the springs. And you'll spread your wings, and you'll be strong again."

"Lowell..." She reached out, but her hand passed through him. "Please don't—"

"You'll heal, Jena. I want that for you. I want you to be strong." Lowell cast longing eyes toward the darkened car where his sons still slept. "I want that for them. This is where they belong, too."

"You're leaving me," she whispered. "You're leaving me, aren't you?"

Her husband's ghost smiled and nodded toward the car. Pulled by some ancient instinct, Jena walked over, opened the door, and got in. The low hum of the engine greeted her, along with her children's quiet snores as she pulled the car back onto the road.

She drove slowly for a few miles. No passing car marred the peace of their journey. Jena put her hand on the center console, and Lowell's ghostly hand hovered over it as she made the left turn off the highway. Her eyes were dry when she spotted the blue sign.

Welcome to Cambio Springs.

She curled her fingers as if to hold onto the last, insubstantial piece of him. For a moment, Lowell's green eyes lifted to hers, and he smiled.

Jena opened her mouth to protest helplessly. "Don't…"

He winked at her one final time, then disappeared, and Jena heard his voice whisper in her ear, "Welcome home, Jena Crowe."

She blinked back tears as she drove through the silent streets. At the edge of town, she passed The Cave, the Campbell's bar, which had been serving beer and guarding the gates of Cambio Springs for as long as anyone could remember. She passed Ollie's giant ranch house a half a mile past, then a few more dark houses. Then a few closer together. She passed the small library where Allie volunteered. City Hall. Ted's clinic. McCann's farm supply. Then, at the signal, she turned right and drove past The Blackbird Diner. It looked like her dad had repainted the sign since the last time they'd visited.

As she slowed down on the next block, she could see the lights on the front porch of her parent's house glowing. A thin figure rose from the porch swing, and the door began to open. Jena heard the boys stir as she pulled into her parents' driveway.

"Mama," Low mumbled. "We home?"

Jena blinked back tears when she saw her father's broad shoulders emerge from the house. His hair was black as midnight, and his eyes as dark as hers. Her mother came to stand beside him, her neck craning to look for the boys in the backseat as Jena brought the car to a stop and put it in park. "Yeah, Low. We're home."

Her son's green eyes met hers in the rearview mirror and locked. Then he nodded once and heaved a quiet sigh. "Okay." He sat up and blinked as he nudged his brother. "Hey, Bear, wake up. We're home."

six
day three

Cambio Springs

HER MOTHER SAT on the edge of her bed, and Jena could feel her stroking the hair back from her forehead before she even opened her eyes. She took a deep breath and woke. The window of her childhood room was cracked open to let in the cool night air, and the sky still wore the pearly light of a newborn day.

She cleared her throat and looked up at her mother. "The boys still asleep?"

Cathy Crowe nodded, her delicate hand falling away from her daughter's forehead. "They'll sleep for a while. They were exhausted."

"Thanks for waking me up."

"No problem." Cathy nodded toward the window. "You going out for a while?"

"Just for a little bit. I want to be back before they wake up."

"Okay." Her mother rose and walked to the door. "Don't lose track of time."

"I'll keep an eye on the sun."

"Okay." Cathy slipped out the door, but her hand held on. She peeked around the corner one last time. "It's good to have you back, sweetie."

"Thanks, Mom."

The door closed, and Jena pushed back the covers. She went to her suitcase and got out her running clothes to change. But instead of putting on the sneakers she'd worn in Oregon, she slipped on a pair of flip-flops. Then Jena Crowe opened the window of her childhood room wide, swung her long legs over the windowsill, and hopped into the garden.

She walked down to the end of the small street on the edge of town where the oldest houses were built, each house resting on a large piece of property that stretched back from the street until it butted up against the red wall of the broad canyon where Cambio Springs had been built. She passed Lowell's parents' house on the right and his aunt and uncle's house on the left, but she kept walking.

Past the houses. Past the park gates. Back to the natural hot springs that lay in a curve of the rocks. The red walls soared up, and green trees lined the base of the cliffs, dipping long branches into the water of the seven springs that dotted the canyon floor. Jena paused, listening as something large rustled in the brush, but she only smiled and continued walking.

Paths had been trimmed and lined, a few of them paved, where the people of the Springs rode bikes, walked, and let the children run in the winter when the days weren't so hot.

Jena passed all of them until she came to a dark slash cut into the canyon wall, where a small stream of water trickled out. She stepped over it and into the ancient cave.

Petroglyphs still marked the walls, high where no human hands should have reached. The sound of steady water filled her ears as she reached over to the niche near the entrance and lit a stubby candle, the low light of dawn not filtering in enough to light her way.

In the back of the cave where the rocks met, water bubbled up out of a sandstone pillar, three feet high, with a basin cut into the top. Like a natural water fountain, the water pushed up out of the rock and trickled over the side, flowing into a small stream that fed into the springs outside. But this water, she knew, wasn't hot and mineral-rich. It would be cool and clear. The water in the cave was the safest and sweetest water in the world.

Jena heard the call of a mockingbird from somewhere outside the cave, and she smiled. Then she took off her sandals and let her feet touch the cool sandstone floor. She slipped off her clothes and put them in another niche cut into the wall. Then, she walked over, bent down, and drank.

The sweet water touched her tongue and slid down her parched throat. Visions of clear skies and open horizons called her. She could almost feel the wind in her face as she took deep, hungry gulps. It splashed over her face, wetting her chin and cheeks, meeting the hot, salty tears that flowed from her eyes. Then Jena took one last desperate draught before her knees gave out. She knelt on the floor, pressing her body into the cold sandstone pillar, hugging it as she wept in sorrow and relief. She felt the water spill over her arms, and she crawled to where it flowed over the side of the basin, curling her naked body under the stream, letting the water soak her skin as she watched the sky at the mouth of the cave grow lighter.

"Don't lose track of time."

She rose, standing tall in the shadows of the cave where generations of others like her had found comfort and strength. She felt the water soak her veins, reaching into a long-hidden part of her soul. She closed her eyes and felt the cool, morning air around her and the water splashing her feet. Then Jena stretched out her arms and let her head fall forward in surrender.

The unbearable lightness started in her heart, which began beating rapidly. The bones in her body felt insubstantial as if the air around her was leaching through her

skin, filling her up. It crept through her limbs and down to her toes as she followed the path of the slick sandstone where the ancient spring led her into the cool morning air. Jena felt the light touch her face and the wind lift her arms.

Then she raised her head, opened her eyes, and wasn't.

The russet-feathered hawk spread its wings and leaped into the morning air, letting out a shriek as it flew over the town. It pumped its wings, catching the current of air that streamed through the canyon as it flew higher and higher over the desert floor. It dipped and climbed, arching over the trees, the houses, and the rocks that spread out for miles around them.

The hawk kept one watchful eye on the angle of the sun as it flew over the desert. Then Jena Crowe let out another piercing cry and soared.

five mornings

One morning can change everything. Five mornings can change a life.

Alex McCann and Teodora 'Ted' Vasquez never had a simple relationship... but you couldn't call it a boring one either.

Friends. Lovers. Enemies. Allies.

Five mornings in their past shape who they will become to each other. To their families. And to the mysterious town they call home.

one
the first morning

VENICE BEACH, *California*
2001

He was finally where he wanted to be. Curled around her, he listened to the waves out the window of the crappy little apartment he'd rented in Venice. It was only one room, and the carpet smelled like shit, but after last night, Alex decided that one room wasn't so bad. After they'd tumbled through the door of the apartment the night before, lips never parting, devouring each other as they ripped off clothing, the bed had only been a few steps away. A few steps to put him exactly where he'd wanted to be.

Next to her for the rest of his life.

He curled his body around her as she slept, arm around her waist, his large hand held her breast as he felt the slow, steady beat of her heart against his thumb. They were nice breasts. He'd wanted to get his hands on them since he first noticed in junior high. It was like they'd appeared out of nowhere one day. A present for the hormonal thirteen-year-old boys of Cambio Springs.

Alex realized even then he'd probably just been a thirteen-year-old idiot who sometimes forgot the tomboy who lived down the street was a girl. The breasts had improved with age, and now they felt perfect against his palms. They tasted just as good. His head bent, and he touched his tongue to the curve of her neck, brushing the tangled black hair away until his lips were against her skin.

Alex heard her sigh in her sleep, and she murmured something unintelligible. He saw the corner of her lip curl up as if she was getting ready to rip into him again, and he smiled as he kissed her neck.

Arguing over margaritas and socialized medicine the night before. She'd taken the night off from studying when he insisted on dragging her away from her dorm. It was a call from Allie that did it.

Ted didn't get out enough. Her friends were worried. She was stressed about the MCAT. He was the closest to her. She needed a familiar voice. A friend.

He and Ted had never been friends.

Since the moment she'd curled her lip at him in freshman biology when she'd been forced to be his lab partner, they hadn't been friends.

"You're such a slacker, Alex."

She would say they were friends like she didn't catch his eyes watching her. Like she didn't know his teasing had another layer. For seven years, they'd danced around it, and he'd waited. Alex McCann didn't wait for much, but he'd make an exception for Teodora Vasquez. Because from that moment in biology class, he'd known.

She was his. And he was hers.

It only took seven years, countless arguments, and a few margaritas to break through.

She stretched in his arms and turned to her back, opening her body to him. He took the advantage, holding her loosely as he let his mouth trail from her neck down to her collar bone, the warm tan skin starting to glow from the light coming through the window. In a few moments, the sun would break through the thin curtains and light her up. He waited, still holding her as she slowly woke.

"Mmmm."

The light crossed the closed lids of her eyes, and they fluttered open, blinking in confusion for a second before they warmed with recognition. He lifted his mouth from her skin and smiled.

"Call me a slacker," he whispered.

She grinned a sleepy smile that turned into a yawn as she stretched her arms over her head, grabbing onto the metal bars of his cheap bed before they came down again and rested on his shoulders.

"After last night, I may have to reconsider your slacker status," she mumbled.

Her voice was low and hoarse in the mornings, and Alex loved that he knew that now. Loved that he knew how her back arched when he went down on her. Loved the hitching breath she took right before she came. He'd learn every cue. Every sign. Like he'd studied exactly how much he could tease her before she blew up at him. Exactly how far she'd take an argument before she retreated into sullen silence. She may have been the star student, the brains behind their little cadre of friends, but Alex had been a student of Ted for years.

"Téa..." He whispered before he kissed her. He didn't give a shit about morning breath, his or hers. He just had to kiss her again. She might try to pull away from the night before, try to walk away like she'd walked away from all the other guys before him. Not too close. Never too close. A little fun, a little company, and then Ted walked away before the secrets came out.

But he knew her secrets. Every single one. And he also knew that neither of them would walk away from this, not without scars that scored deep.

His kiss grew and held until, finally, he felt her hands dig into his shoulders, her little cat claws coming out to grip his skin.

Dig in, baby. That's just where I want you.

He shifted her under him, moving until his hips were between her thighs, then he felt her legs come up and press in.

Yep. She was exactly where she wanted to be, too.

He was a gentleman, so he tried not to crow in triumph. Besides, he had better things to do.

She was panting when he pulled his mouth away.

"Do you have another—"

"Yes." He reached for the bedside table.

"Hurry, Alex."

"Always in such a rush, Téa." He grinned as he rolled the condom on and then paused, waiting for her eyes to come back to his. They locked with his as he slowly edged inside. "Slow down, baby," he murmured against her lips. "I'm not going anywhere."

"Alex..." She wasn't quite so chatty when he was

making love to her. Ted could argue about anything. The economy. The price of gas. The best tequila. The proper way to drink that tequila. But when he was inside her, when they were moving together, she'd been quiet.

Best way to shut her up, ever.

"Téa," he groaned, sinking into her body again and again; he felt it. The same feeling he'd had the night before. The first time. The only time that meant anything, really.

Because it had always been Téa. She was home.

The only sound in the room was the tide coming in and their breathing. He said nothing to her. She said nothing to him. There was nothing to say. This had been building for years. Every step he'd taken had circled around her. Every move he'd made had been unconsciously coming closer. Until she was there. Right where he'd always wanted her.

"Baby, I'm gonna—"

"Yes."

It was the only word she'd said.

Yes. Yes. Yes.

She could say it a thousand times, and he'd never tire of it.

Yes, Alex.

Yes, we're here.

Yes, finally.

This is right. This has always been.

Yes.

When she came, she arched her back, and he buried his face in her neck as her body gripped his. Holding on.

Please, hold on.

He pushed up, bracing his arms at her sides as he

pushed toward his own release. She reached down, short nails digging into his hips as he drove her.

"Téa," he groaned out as he felt it rising. He was there. Her eyes grew soft and warm. Her fingers dug in deeper as she said it again.

"Yes."

He came in a rush, the lightning pulse of release throwing him over the edge as he pushed into her over and over. And she held on. Through the hard crush of his body when he collapsed onto her. Through the fierce kisses, he pressed against her neck. Her face. Her mouth. His hands were tangled in her hair. He didn't want to let go, so he didn't. He just rolled to the side, and she came with him, locking her legs around his hips even as he slid out of her. Parted but still together.

Alex was breathing heavy when he finally broke away. He gathered her into his arms, and she came to him, pressing her cheek to his heart so her breath tickled the hair on his chest, and he could feel the flush of her skin. He held her like that as the sun rose. The room smelled like salt air and sex and her. He didn't notice the musty smell of the old carpet his landlord refused to replace. He just smelled *them*.

Best scent ever.

After a few minutes, she cleared her throat, and Alex smiled, knowing that Quiet Ted was history.

For a while.

"So, I'll revise my judgment of slacker. At least in one area."

His hand slid down to her ass and cupped it, and his tongue licked under her chin. "Only one?"

"One area with several disciplines."

He laughed and hugged her tighter. "There's my Ted."

"You didn't call me Ted last night. Or this morning." Her eyes met his, and he saw them spark. "When did I become 'Téa?'"

"I'm not going to shout out 'Ted, oh Ted!' when I come. Forget it."

She lifted an eyebrow and considered him.

"Besides," he said, brushing a kiss over her pursed lips. "Ted is a hard-ass, sharp as a whip, take no prisoners, almost-med student who's going to be a kickass doctor someday. But Téa—" He kissed her again and trailed his fingers up and down her back. "—is soft and silk when she purrs. She's quiet and giving." The corner of his lip curled up. "Very giving."

She rolled her eyes and tried to pull away, but he didn't let her.

"Alex—"

"You can be both," he whispered into her hair. She stilled immediately. "With me, you can be both. Always my Ted. And my Téa. You can be both, baby. With me."

She pulled her head away so she could look into his eyes. "Your Téa?"

"This is it, Ted. You know it is. This was always going to be. So yeah. My Téa. And my Ted. I wouldn't have one without the other, baby."

"Don't call me 'baby.'"

"I'm gonna call you 'baby' until the day I die. And you're gonna hate it. And I'm not going to care because the makeup sex will be hot as hell."

He saw her trying not to laugh, so he kissed her again, and when he pulled away, she was smiling.

"This changes everything, doesn't it, Alex McCann?"

"Absolutely." He rolled over and pulled her to rest on his chest. She was stiff for a moment like she didn't know whether he could take her weight. Then she relaxed into him, and he let out the breath he'd been holding.

"Yes."

two
the second morning

LOS ANGELES, *CA*

2003

"They're going to expect you to be there."

"I understand that." Ted was slamming books and folders into her backpack, clearly displeased they were having this conversation again. "And I also realize that I have an exam that day I cannot miss."

"You could leave after it." Alex talked around the bite of cereal he was downing before he started the drive to Orange County and the construction site he was working on. "You'd be late, but you'd be there."

"And then the ceremony will go until midnight. At least. And you have to stay, so I'd have to drive myself back for three hours on little to no sleep and probably end up missing class or getting into a wreck."

She didn't even look at him. Ted had a plan for that semester, and Alex's grandfather passing away didn't fit into it. They'd both made it out for the funeral, but the town meeting where Alex's father would officially take over a seat on the Elder's Council fit into her schedule even less than a funeral did.

"You know," she muttered, "I don't have a job with a boss who thinks I walk on water, Alex. Who will let me out of work because I have 'family issues.' I'm a nobody med student who has to play by the rules, or I get creamed. By professors. By my classmates. You have no idea how hard this is."

It never failed to infuriate him. As if they hadn't been living together for a year. He'd put up with her relentless schedule because he loved her. And because he knew it wasn't forever.

"This is important." He set down the bowl on the counter and crossed his arms. "My dad is taking over the clan and pack leadership. This happens once every thirty years. If that. And you're telling me that you can't make the drive and sacrifice for the family when—"

"It's not *my* family!"

"It will be!"

Her furious black eyes met his, but she said nothing. She knew it was true.

Family had always been the sticking point, and it always would be. Neither one of their families approved of their relationship. Teodora Vasquez was directly in line to head the clan of feline shapeshifters that made Cambio Springs their home. She was a powerful mountain lion and the most dominant animal in her generation. The fact that she was female was only a bonus to the primarily matriarchal cat shifters. The current clan leadership consisted of her grandfather and a distant great-aunt. When Ted's mother took over, it would put both the cat elder seats in female hands, the way the cats liked it.

Which made Alex her equal and opposite in every possible way. The oldest, most dominant of the McCann wolf shifters in his generation, there was no question who would take over when his father resigned from the council or died. He was the clear alpha, and Robert McCann had made no secret of the fact that he expected his son to take over pack leadership when his years had passed. The other McCann wolf on the council was there for his vote, and that was it. There was only one alpha of the Cambio wolves, and everyone acknowledged that Alex would be it.

Their families fought like cats and dogs. Literally.

And Alex still knew that Ted was the only woman in the world for him.

"They'll be your family someday, Ted. We're already fighting an uphill battle on this. You showing up would help. A lot."

"The entire rest of my family will be there."

"But you, the future wife of their pack leader, will not. And if you think no one will notice, you're kidding yourself." Alex didn't miss that it was the first time he'd pulled out the 'wife' card, even though they both knew where they were going. They'd known from the beginning.

For the first time, he saw Ted's pain behind her frustration and anger.

"Don't do that."

"Do what?"

"Bring that up when we're fighting. That is not the time to bring it up, Alex."

"I think it's the perfect time to bring it up because you

always manage to skirt around it and how it's going to affect our future. My family and pack are part of our future, Ted."

"If that's true, then they're going to have to get used to it. To me. I'm not a submissive little she-wolf who—"

"Don't even go there!" he said, steaming. "You do not get how pack hierarchy works, so do not insult submissives that way. And you know it has nothing to do with sex. There are just as many female—"

"Dominants? No, there aren't, Alex! You're kidding yourself if you think that. And I know what they all think about me. About us together. The uppity cat—"

"Lower your voice," he hissed, glancing at the walls around them.

"Don't tell me what to do." She still lowered her voice, just as conscious of their need for secrecy among so many strangers. "They don't like me. I get that. They don't think I'm a good partner for you. I get that, too. Do you really think me showing up and smiling at your dad's ceremony is going to help?"

"I can't hurt for them to know you think the town is a priority. That tradition is still important."

"A priority?" she choked out the word, and he didn't miss the angry tears that shone in her eyes. "They question whether I think the Springs is a priority?"

"Not me. Never me. And not my mom or dad, either."

"Don't they realize?" she asked. "I'm doing this for *them*. For the town. For all of our families."

"They know that, baby."

"You just said they don't."

Cambio Springs had never had a doctor. Alex's great-aunt had been a nurse during World War II, and she ran a clinic out of her kitchen, but that was as close as the town had ever had to native medical care. The rest of them risked driving into Indio to see doctors when they had the rare injury, hoping the doctors didn't notice how quickly they healed and how resistant they were to painkillers of any kind. Ted was the first shifter with the academic credentials and inclination to go to medical school. And she was the only one willing to put up with the grueling schedule.

"Do they think I like being out here?" she asked. "Away from home? Working my ass off at school and my job and missing my family?"

He uncrossed his arms and went to her but didn't miss her quick glance at the clock. Alex knew that, even as close as they lived to campus, she was going to have to hustle not to be late with traffic. He still took a moment to fold her in his arms and kiss the top of her head.

"They don't know because they can't. And you're not a complainer, so they take your hard work for granted. I understand that."

And if Alex felt like Ted took him for granted some-times, he'd live with it. It wasn't the most important thing that morning. And it wouldn't be forever. He knew that, too.

"I have... *five more years* of this, Alex. At least. Five more years of work like this. Of living like shit so I can keep my loans to a minimum. And at the end of all of it, I'm going to end up in a town in the middle of the desert where I'll probably be paid in eggs and yard work more than cash."

"I have money."

And he'd have more. He was a quick learner, and construction work wasn't going to make him the kind of money he needed to make if he wanted to pull his hometown out of poverty. Alex was watching the real estate market. Watching closely. People were way overextended, and a crash was coming soon. Bad for homeowners but good for people looking for the right opportunity.

He'd studied what his boss did and knew that he could make more. Renovating existing real estate and flipping it wasn't a TV show for him. He knew he could do it, and he knew he could make money. A lot of it, if he played his cards right.

Alex was a damn good card player.

"You can't pay off all my loans, Alex. And besides, my mom and grandpa—"

"Are gonna pay part of it. Yeah, I know. And you've already got a ton of financial aid. But you know I'm right, and it won't matter once we're married, so suck it up, Vasquez. I'm helping you out."

"You already pay more than your share of the rent."

"We're having this argument again?" He tilted her chin up and smiled at her pursed lips. Every time she made that face, he wanted to kiss her.

So he did. Then he slid his hand down her back and gave her ass a quick squeeze before he released her. "You're going to be late for your lab if you don't leave now."

"Shit!" She spun and finished slamming her books into the crammed backpack. "I'll call my mom later and let her know—"

"And I'll call my dad."

"He won't understand." He could hear the frustration and the sadness in her voice. She masked it with anger, but

Alex could always hear the sadness. Scent it on her. See it in her shoulders and around her eyes.

"I'll make him understand. And in the end, it doesn't matter, does it?"

He walked her to the door and hooked a finger around her belt loop, pulling her in for another quick kiss and nuzzling into her neck the way he knew her cat loved.

"Alex, I'm late...."

"I'm the one marrying you, not them."

The sadness left her eyes. "You're really gonna marry me, wolf?"

"Never doubt it for a minute, baby."

She rolled her eyes and stepped to the door. "Don't call me baby."

Alex slapped her ass and opened the door. "You love it."

"No, I don't," she called down the hall.

"I love you, baby." He was grinning when she started down the stairs.

"I love you, too." And Alex laughed when he heard her muttering, "Asshole...."

three
the third morning

SANTA MONICA, *CA*

2006

"What do you mean you're not coming?"

They were in bed, one of the few quiet mornings they'd had together in months. Alex could hear it again, the ocean coming in from the window, just like his old apartment in Venice. Ted was next to him, only this time, she wasn't sleepy and satisfied.

She was confused.

"I can't." He was almost whispering. Forcing the words out of his mouth. He knew exactly how much it would hurt her because he'd been living with a gut wound for months, ever since she'd gotten the acceptance to Eisenhower.

She could have gone anywhere. Ted's hard work had paid off. She'd graduated in the top five percent of her class. Had acceptance at some of the finest teaching hospitals in California. She was taking a residency in Palm Springs to be closer to family. Closer to the Springs.

And Alex just told her he wasn't coming with her.

"What do you mean you *can't*?" Her voice dropped from high and shocked to deadly serious. "This was always the plan. We live out here while I'm in school. We move home when we're done. I'm *done*. Or almost done. Finally done, and you're telling me—"

"Your plan, Ted." Her eyes widened, but he kept going. "*Your* plan. It's always been your plan. Did you stop once, in the five years we've been together, and ask me what *my* plan was?"

"I thought your plan—"

"Was to follow you around for eight years while you pursued your dreams and I ignored my own?"

Her mouth dropped open, and his heart sank.

She'd never even considered it. Alex wondered if she'd even noticed at all.

He was finally doing it. He was finally making money. Real money. The kind of money that could lead to huge opportunities for his family, his pack, and his town. He sold three houses in his first year. He sold ten the year after that. And it was only getting bigger. Banks were foreclosing, letting homes go for a song. He was picking them up, brushing them off with the crew he'd built, and selling them for enough profit to invest in the next two or three with money to spare. He'd worked his ass off, and he was finally setting money aside. Single homes would lead to investment properties like apartment complexes and commercial real estate. And he was making connections with the people who moved things in Southern California. Finally getting in on deals he'd only looked at from afar.

And the love of his life was moving to Palm Springs.

"I can't leave now, Téa." He kept talking, even though the gut wound only bled faster. "I can't. I have to stay here."

"I promised my mom. My grandpa. I need to be closer. I can finally see them more than a few times a year. Finally—"

"I understand. You have to go."

He did know. She'd been away from the Springs for too long. Eight years. The last four almost without a break. She hardly ever shifted, and her cat was growing restless. Alex had come home more than one night to find a mountain lion snarling and pacing through their small apartment. Hard sex tired her out. It helped, but it wasn't enough. In the last year, she'd begun shifting in her sleep, which was a bad sign. She needed to be closer to home, and he couldn't go with her.

A small, resentful part of him didn't want to.

It wasn't the distance. It was the fact that through everything—the late nights, the exams, the constant, constant stress of medical school—when he'd made her schedule and her dreams a priority, she hadn't even asked about his.

Not once.

She'd sometimes ask him casually what he was doing at work. Half the time, she was asleep before he finished answering.

"But you don't have to stay here, Alex. You can work from anywhere. Construction jobs—"

"Do you really think I work construction?" He sat up in bed and looked down at her. "Really? That's what you've boiled my business down to? Construction?"

"But you said—"

"You haven't listened to a word I've said in three fucking years, Ted."

Her eyes narrowed, and she sat up in bed next to him, wrapping the sheet around her body. He didn't blame her. Despite the sunshine peeking in through the window, the bedroom felt unbearably cold.

"You decided this without me," she said.

"Like you haven't made every single decision in your life without consulting me? You didn't even ask me when you were considering residencies. Not once. You could have gone anywhere."

Her eyes flashed. "You don't think I know that? I picked Eisenhower because—"

"It's close to home. I realize that."

"And you have no idea how much I need to go home."

"You think I don't?"

"Of course not! You're there for a long weekend two times a month! You see your mom and dad and your sister as much as you want. And you get to run. And spend time with our friends. And—"

"And you've always said no. Even when you did have the time, you said—"

"I never had the time!"

"You could have made the time if it was important, Ted. You could have made time for your family so you didn't burn yourself out. You might even have made the time for me! But that would have been too much of an inconvenience, wouldn't it?"

"You want a woman who'll follow you around like—"

"You! I want *you*, Ted! But that was just too much to give, wasn't it? You could give yourself to everything in your life, but you didn't have any left to give me, did you?"

He couldn't cry. He wouldn't, even though he could feel the burning at the corner of his eye. Alex felt like he was ripping off his own skin. His wolf clawed at him, angry to be away from the mate it had come to need. The animal inside urged him to go to her. Put his arms around her. Give her whatever she wanted so they could be together.

But the man held back.

Finally, he held back.

"It's not just you, Alex. It never has been. It never will be."

His father's words haunted him. Not because they made him angry—even though they did—but because they were true.

He didn't only live for himself. He was a leader. The future leader of a family, a pack, a town. When he worked, it was for them. When he planned, he planned for them. And when a dream had to be sacrificed, his was the first one to go. Because that's what being a leader meant. That much his father had always taught him. Not power. Not glory. Leadership meant sacrifice. Family first. Pack first.

It wasn't just him. It never would be.

She stared at him, speechless, her heart breaking in her eyes. She hadn't held back the tears. Not his Ted. She held back nothing. When she was angry, she told him off. When she was happy, she soared. She held nothing back in passion. Her heart had always been open to him.

And Alex was breaking it.

"I need to stay here, Ted. I need to see this through. My work is here, not out in the desert. I can't go with you. Not now."

She finally choked out, "When?"

"I don't know."

"A year? Two years?"

"I don't know."

"Five years?"

"I don't—"

"Six?"

"I told you, I don't—"

"Give me something!" she screamed. "Give me *something*, Alex!"

The tears were pouring down her face. He clenched his hands together to keep from grabbing her and running. He'd grab her, and they'd both run. Away from responsibilities. Away from family obligations and history that haunted them. Away from every family member that had predicted this inevitable day.

"Tell me," she choked out. "Give me... something."

She wanted a deadline. She wanted a promise.

Three years will be enough.

Five years and we'll be together.

Alex shook his head. "I don't know."

"All this time," she said. "All this time, you knew this was coming. For months, you knew."

"Yes."

"And you said nothing."

There was no response. She was right. He could blame her for not asking, but he'd held off talking to her because he knew how it would end. He'd held on to the small bit of herself Ted had given him for as long as he could have it.

Their lease ran out at the end of the month, and they hadn't signed another.

Because she was going back to the desert.

And he could go to hell.

She whispered, "If you love me—"

"Don't." He grabbed her hand, desperate for her to not finish the ultimatum. "Baby, please."

Alex pulled her toward him, holding onto her hand as he bent down and pressed his forehead against hers.

Don't say it. Don't make me choose. Don't close the door and lock it.

Please.

Please.

Please.

"If you love me," she whispered, "you'll come with me."

He closed his eyes and dropped her hand, stepping away from her touch.

That was Ted. Black and white. Fiercely loyal and utterly uncompromising. She'd be a powerful clan leader someday.

What she wouldn't be, was *his*.

He nodded silently. His jaw clenched so he didn't loose his rage. He wanted to break something. He wanted to put his fist through a wall. He wanted to break every plate in their kitchen and tear up the sheets that still smelled like them. Throw the bed against the wall and pound his fists in the door.

So he did nothing while she walked from the room.

Ten minutes later, he walked out of the bedroom, dressed in his work clothes. Ted was sitting at the counter, still wrapped in a sheet, drinking coffee with a blank look on her face. If she were anyone else, he'd worry about leaving her alone. But she wasn't anyone else; she was Ted.

He forced his voice to be smooth and controlled. "I'll get my stuff out when you're at the hospital later today. I can stay with Joey for a while."

Ted said nothing.

If he touched her, he'd break. So Alex walked out the door and didn't look back.

four
the fourth morning

PALM SPRINGS, *California*

2008

He didn't know why he drove to her house. He knew where she lived, of course. All their friends knew, just as they knew to avoid the subject of Ted when he was around. He saw her. Rarely. When he was in town, she made herself scarce. Easy to do when she worked as much as she did. According to their friend Jena, her residency was going well, and she'd already set up a clinic in town. It was off the books, but it was better than nothing. The rest of her time was spent at the hospital or at a small house she was renting nearby.

Alex didn't know if she was dating anyone. Didn't know if she'd tried to move on or if the results had been as soul-sucking as his own. He'd tried to date, which was absurd. But he'd been so angry, he had to try. A few disastrous dates and a one-night stand later, he'd given up. He woke up the next day feeling like shit; his wolf clawed his skin.

He missed her so damn much.

Two years they spent avoiding each other, even when he was in Palm Springs, overseeing the renovations to the office complex he'd bought seven months before. It was eight in the morning, and he'd spent another sleepless night, knowing she was close but out of his reach. He was exhausted when he pulled up to the small bungalow she rented. He parked on the street and leaned back in his seat to close his eyes.

Enough. It was enough to be this close. Closer than he'd been since they'd both attended their friend Lowell's memorial service the year before.

He drifted to sleep but woke up when he heard a tapping on the window.

She was there, staring at him with equally exhausted eyes, her car in the driveway. She looked the same, though her hair was a little shorter than the last time he'd seen her. The lines around her eyes were deeper, but he knew it was the lack of sleep. She'd looked the same around exams every semester. He rolled down the window.

"You just going to sleep here? It's going to be over a hundred in an hour, and you'll roast, even in this fancy car."

Alex said nothing. He didn't know what to say. He hadn't thought ahead that far.

She sighed and opened the car door. "Come inside, Alex."

He did what she told him, taking the hand she held out, not even letting it drop when she unlocked the front door and walked into the dim house. The shades were pulled to fight against the relentless desert heat. Even in April, it would be over a hundred degrees by mid-morning. They were both silent as she led him around the house.

"Shoes." She pointed toward the door, and he toed them off near the neat line of sandals that waited there. "Pockets." She didn't wait for him but gently patted his pockets, knowing he kept an assortment of keys, an over-stuffed wallet, and various receipts stuffed there. She pulled it all out and set it in an orderly line on the kitchen counter. Undid his belt and set it next to the wallet. Then she pulled him down the hall, still holding his hand while he said nothing, fighting exhaustion and the urge to wrap her in his arms and not let go. Her shoulders were stooped. She was as exhausted as he was.

They walked into a room that, Alex noted absently, was about as personal as a hotel room. No pictures. No frilly pillows or art on the wall. It was a place to sleep, not her home. It didn't come as a surprise. He'd always been the one to decorate when they'd lived together. Her home was the Springs. Any place other than that was just a rest stop on the road back.

"Jeans," she said quietly. He took off his jeans—dusty from the job site because he needed to do laundry—leaving him in her bedroom in nothing but a t-shirt and boxers.

She pushed him toward the bed, and he sat, immediately feeling lightheaded. He hadn't slept well in a month. Not since he'd come out here to look over the finish work on the property. He'd avoided Palm Springs for as long as he could for that very reason, knowing he'd never find any peace being so close to her and still out of touch.

Ted pushed his shoulders down to the bed that smelled like her.

"Sleep."

He didn't let her hand go.

"I'll grab the couch. It's comfortable enough. I've just come off two days on call, so I'll be dead to the—"

"I miss you."

His voice was hoarse. Unused. As if every conversation he'd had in the two years since he'd spoken to her didn't count. Two years since they'd spoken words that had broken everything. She didn't say anything. Didn't even look at him. Her eyes were locked on the wall behind him. He gave her hand a slight tug.

"I miss you so damn much, Téa."

The rigid line of her shoulders relaxed, and he pulled her closer. Over his body and onto the bed next to him. He didn't pull down the covers. Just positioned her body in front of his, curling around her and shoving his face into her hair. He closed his eyes and let out a breath when he felt her relax against him.

"Sleep," she said.

"Stay with me."

She waited to answer.

"Okay."

He slept. His wolf stopped itching under his skin and settled, finally next to its mate again.

Alex slept better than he had in two years, wrapped around Ted as the fan over them wafted cool air over their exhausted bodies. His arm lay over her waist, his hand still clutching hers. They slept for hours.

When he woke, she was still there. The drapes let in a sliver of light, allowing him to watch her as she rested. The lines had smoothed from her face, and she looked younger.

The stress was gone, if only for a few hours. He waited, knowing that if he moved, she would wake up. She needed the sleep, so he waited. They hadn't moved while they slept. Her back was still tucked up to his front, and her hand was clutched in his. He ignored the inevitable erection that strained against the front of his boxers. Alex had her scent in his nose; his body didn't care how long they'd been apart or what their relationship had become.

He closed his eyes and listened to her breathe. It might have been hours or minutes later. He didn't know, except that the angle of the sun had changed enough so that the beam poured across her face, and she turned toward him. He pressed his lips to her hair. Then her temple.

Her eyes fluttered open, but she didn't move away. So Alex kept kissing her. The arch of her cheekbone. The line of her jaw. His tongue licked out under her chin, tasting salt and skin. He let go of her hand and put his palm on her belly where her scrubs parted to show the line of tan skin at her waist. He sucked in a breath and shoved his face into her neck, waiting. Scenting her desire. His own.

Ted didn't say anything, but he felt her nod against his cheek, and she pulled the drawstring on the pants she wore. He let out a breath and let his hand trail up, cupping her breast under her shirt, shoving the fabric away to get to her skin.

It was silent. The only sound, the soft hush of clothes disappearing. He didn't kiss her mouth. Didn't let himself until he was sliding inside the heat of her body. Then his mouth took hers, ignoring the tears on her cheeks. Ignoring everything but the desperate hunger that captured them both. Her first climax came quickly, and he slowed, determined to stretch the fragile peace they'd come to for as long as he could.

He kissed the tears from her skin, bit the lobe of her ear, and licked behind it the way she loved. It was an old dance, all the more precious for its familiarity. He loved her for as long as he could. Held her tight until he couldn't hold back the climax anymore. Until she bit his neck where it met his shoulder and sent him over the edge.

He groaned into her mouth but didn't leave her body. Not even when he rolled to the side. He stayed with her and didn't let go. He let go of her mouth but kissed every inch of her skin within reach until he felt his eyes begin to droop. She held on as tightly as he did, her arms around his waist and her head tucked into his chest. He could feel her heart race against his skin as he dropped heavy into sleep.

ALEX WOKE TO AN EMPTY BED. Ted's scrubs lay on the floor beside the bed, and the drawer that held more was hanging open. The mirror he could see in the bathroom still held an edge of fog from the shower. Not a sound from the kitchen or the hall. She'd gone back to the hospital while he slept.

He lay in bed for a few minutes, then sat up and pulled on his jeans. The sky was dark outside, and the room was cooler, the temperature in the desert dropping with the sun. He walked down the hall and headed for the kitchen where she'd put his things. There was a note and a key lying by his wallet.

Alex, I'm back on at nine, so I had to go. Please lock up. You can put the extra key under the mat. —Ted

He picked up the key, staring at the shiny, unused brass that lay in his palm. He checked his phone and saw a text message from an unknown number. Desert area code. He clicked on it and stared at the message he knew must have come from her.

When are you coming home?

He knew she was talking about the Springs. Knew she was looking for that timeline again. A timeline he couldn't give her. It would be a promise. And Alex didn't break promises. Ever. So he never made those he knew he couldn't keep.

He closed his eyes and rested his elbows on the counter, staring at the message from the only woman he'd ever loved, asking a question he couldn't answer. The weight of expectations hung on his shoulders. He was over halfway there. He thought. But he didn't know. So he picked up his phone and sent her the only answer he had.

Soon.

Then Alex palmed her key and stuffed his wallet and keys back in his pocket. He got a quick drink of water and put the glass in the empty dishwasher. He slipped his shoes on, locked up, and dropped the key in his pocket, smiling a little as he walked to the car.

Ted may want her door locked, but Alex wasn't leaving without a key.

five
the fifth morning

CAMBIO SPRINGS, *California*

2010

He didn't shift when the car pulled away. It was a sheriff's cruiser, and Alex had pissed on every tire as soon as he'd shown up at her house. Then he paced in the stand of cottonwood at the edge of her property.

Paced for hours.

She stood in the doorway, watching the early sun flash on the chrome light rack of Dev's car. The pink morning glow hit the side of her house, which he knew she'd painted the summer she moved in. Clean whitewash over old adobe. It was a solid house, even though it was old.

Alex paced, and a low growl rumbled from his throat. He saw her eyes whip toward the trees, and her nose lifted in the cool air.

He loped out of the house in wolf form, still too furious to change back to human. His lip curled when he saw her face.

It told him nothing. When once, it would have told him everything.

She stared, glancing between the dust of the retreating car and the massive timber wolf that stalked her yard. Pulling her robe a little tighter around herself, she squared her shoulders at him and said, "Shift or get out of here."

Alex shifted but didn't stop pacing. Light paw steps became heavy footfalls as he walked from one end of her front yard to the other, ignoring the brambles that cut his feet. Ignoring the pain in his chest. Ignoring the cool breeze that bit his bare skin.

"Stop it, Alex."

His lip curled again, and he stopped. Right in front of her. He glared up at her, clenching his fists and resisting the urge to grab her and haul her back into the house that Devin Moon had just left.

Dev. Not some idiot resident she had a fling with. Dev. Not some casual acquaintance she'd forget about in a month. Dev. Who knew her secrets. Their secrets. Dev, who had always teased Ted and flirted with her, even when it pissed her off.

"What was he doing here?"

She closed her eyes and sighed. "What do you think, Alex? Were you here all night?"

"No. Just about the time that Joey let slip at the Cave that you've been seeing him."

Her mouth twisted in annoyance. "Alex—"

"Is he your boyfriend?"

"None of your business."

He took a step up. "None of my business?"

The blank look fell from her face, and she snarled, "This

is the most you've spoken to me in two years. You tell me you're coming home 'soon,' then for two years, I barely see you. We never talk about what happened—"

"What was there to say?"

Her mouth dropped open, but she said nothing. His anger was still riding him. He wanted to tear into her house and wipe every trace of the other man from her room. Cover her body with his until Dev was nothing but a hazy memory. He wanted...

He wanted Ted. More than anything, he wanted Ted. And she was yet another thing just out of his reach.

"Wh—what was there to say?" she asked.

"You know why I'm in LA. You know why I can't tell you when I'm moving back." He stepped up again until he was right in front of her. Naked. Angry. Let her try to ignore him. Let her try to hide. "And you know how I feel about you. You always have."

"It's over, Alex. It was over four years—"

He didn't let her finish. Alex swooped down and took her mouth in a bruising kiss. She opened to him like they'd spent minutes apart, not years. He grabbed onto her, clutching one hand at her waist as another dug into her hair and held. She tasted like coffee and toothpaste. She tasted like Ted in the morning after he'd woken her up with his mouth. She tasted like home.

Alex stopped his relentless assault on her mouth when the pain registered. His heart hurt. His groin ached with needing her. And Ted was gripping his bicep so hard he figured she'd leave bruises. He didn't care.

"You and me?" he finally said. "You and me aren't over. We never will be."

❋ 69 ❋

She shook her head. "Why are you here?"

"Just letting you know where we stand, baby."

"Baby?" she hissed, pushing him away. "Shut up. You don't get to come back here whenever you want and try to mess with my love life, Alex. You opted out, *baby*, so go home. To LA. That's where you want to be."

"Your love life?" He stepped back to her. "You in love with him? With Dev?"

If she was, he was screwed. He saw the flush hit her cheeks as her anger swelled into something even more dangerous.

Cold. She could be so cold when she wanted to be.

"What if I am?"

"That's not an answer."

"He's not the first guy I've dated since we broke up."

Alex said nothing. No, Dev wasn't the first, and he couldn't blame her for that, even if he hated it. The fact was, he'd let her go and even tried to move on himself. But when he was back at the Springs, when the wolf came out to play, he knew the truth of the matter.

She was his. He was hers. There would be no other mate but her.

"You know he's not the first. He's just the first that matters, right?" Her eyes started heating up again, and Alex was grateful. Grateful just to be able to get a rise out of her.

"I was—"

"You were pissing on your territory, McCann. You don't want me, but you won't let me move on with any guy who might actually stand a chance, will you?"

"I don't want you?" He ignored the truth in her accusation and focused on the part they both knew wasn't true.

"Who the hell do you think I'm working for, Ted? Who's the one that really matters?"

She shook her head and took another step back into her house; Alex followed.

"You're working for your pack. For your family. I'm not faulting you for it, but—"

"I'm working so this town doesn't shrivel up and die! I want—"

"I know what you want! I want the same thing." She took a deep breath and closed her eyes a moment before she opened them. The anger had drained away. The blank look was back.

Back in perfectly controlled Ted mode. He hated what she was going to say before she even spoke.

"We want the same thing for this place, Alex. There's no avoiding each other. But we both need to move on with our lives."

The cool words cut into his chest like a knife.

"We have history," she continued. "There were hard feelings on both sides. But it's in the past. We're not children. For the good of everyone, we need to—"

"Don't." He grabbed her by the waist and spun her against the wall, pressing her forehead to his the same way he'd done four years before.

"If you love me, you'll come with me."

The memory of her words threatened to choke him.

"Don't say we need to move on. Don't."

"Alex—"

"Give me a little more time, Téa." He whispered the words, afraid of breaking the fragile hold he had on her. "You know what we have. What we could have. You made

※ 71 ※

me choose four years ago, and I made the only choice I could."

He'd been proud. Angry. Hurt. He'd been twenty-seven and an ego-ridden idiot. The four years he'd lived without her had been empty. If he had to do it again, he'd have held onto her like a drowning man on a life raft.

She said nothing, so he kept talking.

"Just... don't do anything permanent. Don't break this."

"Don't *break* this?" He could hear the tears in her voice. "I didn't break this. You did."

If she'd punched him, it couldn't have hurt worse.

"Téa—"

"You broke my heart, Alex. Then you came back and broke it again."

"I know!" he shouted, grabbing her face in his hands. "I know I did. And I'll break it again. And you'll break mine. You're still the only woman in the world I want."

"Don't—"

"Because no one can hurt me the way you do. And no one could ever love me the way you can."

He felt her tears catch on his thumbs and run down the edge between his palm and her flushed cheek.

"Why are you doing this to me?" she whispered.

"Because I love you." He kissed her forehead. "It's only ever been you. And you know it as well as I do."

She turned her head and closed her eyes, letting the tears come. She pushed his hands away from her face. She didn't say anything. She didn't have to. He knew how badly he'd messed things up. He knew what his actions had cost them both. And he knew he'd have a long road back to her arms.

But he could be patient.

Alex stepped away and went to the door. She still had her eyes closed, refusing to look at him. But her need followed him as he walked away.

He turned when he reached the door. "Ted, if you could just—"

"When are you coming home? I want a real answer this time."

Her eyes were still closed, and the sun shone across her face, warming the soft tan to brilliant gold.

"Soon."

A slight twitch at the corner of her mouth told him the answer disappointed her.

"I'll be back, Téa. I promise. As soon as I can."

Then Alex walked out the door and shifted back to his wolf, leaving his heart in an old adobe house in the desert with a woman who could hold it or crush it with a word. He ran through the desert, letting the wolf take him. And every step away from her was the first step of his return.

stings and arrows

Sean Quinn escaped Cambio Springs with nothing but the clothes on his back, fleeing from a scorned clan, an unearned reputation, and the weight of family history.

Wandering the world as a travel photographer suited him, until he met one fellow wanderer who would upset everything he thought about his future.

You can travel the world and hide in different skins, but eventually, someone will see you for exactly who you are.

one
meet me in la

Los Angeles, California

SEAN SPOTTED her through the office's glass walls while he was having coffee with his editor. "Who's the kid?"

Rani glanced up and immediately knew who he was referring to. "She's someone new who did a favor for my boss, which means you have to be nice to her because she's working for pennies and experience."

Sean humph'ed and took a swallow of his coffee, barely keeping himself from spitting it out.

Rani must have seen the pain on his face because she looked amused, and his pain was generally one of her primary sources of amusement. "You know, drinking scalding hot black coffee with no milk or sugar isn't a character trait, Sean. It doesn't make you interesting."

No, but turning into a snake in front of you would probably qualify, right?

He managed to get it down without embarrassing himself more. "I just like black coffee."

"And pretty women." She batted her eyelashes at him. "I'm taken now, so I know you're depressed, but don't hit on the new girl."

He leaned back and smirked. "I would never."

"You would."

"Is it my fault that trust-fund babies like slumming it with the bad boy?"

From almost the instant he became a staff photographer for Distinction International, beautiful women and more than a few men had been angling for his attention.

He knew he was good-looking. It was the blessing and the curse of most Quinn men. That and turning into reptiles on full moon nights.

Sean didn't talk about his poverty-ridden background, so that made him mysterious. He didn't ask many questions because he avoided attachments, which made him aloof.

Good looking, mysterious, and aloof with access to three different print publications, including a leading fashion magazine? He'd spent the first few years working for Distinction with no lack of female company.

Rani leaned forward. "Do you own anything that isn't black?"

"Yes."

"What?"

He glanced at his black jeans and a black t-shirt. With his pale skin and dark hair, he knew it made for an eye-catching combination, but he hadn't started with this uniform as a statement.

Black was cheap and made it easy to hide stains. When he'd been a skinny seventeen-year-old kid on his own, that was important.

"I think I have a pair of khaki pants somewhere." And a few free t-shirts that were almost brand new. "The new girl has florescent pink hair. Don't criticize me about my wardrobe."

"She's not a trust fund kid, as far as I can tell." Rani leaned back and craned her neck to examine the young woman filling out paperwork at a desk across the office. "I assumed she was, but I was told quite bluntly that wasn't the case and we shouldn't ask her about her background. So who knows?" Rani shrugged and moved on to the scattered file spread over her desk. "I like this direction, and I think a new take on Holi in Mathura is a nice idea. Is it overdone, though?"

"I don't think so. At least as far as I can tell, the magazine has covered Holi, but not in the place where its biggest celebration happens."

"It's not really a luxury destination, Sean. And that's the point of this magazine."

If you ask trendsetters, what's selling to younger travelers with funds these days is *authenticity*. This isn't the generation who did their gap year skiing in Switzerland; they were building eco-friendly housing in Brazil, you hear me?"

"While sleeping in five-star accommodations, of course."

Sean rolled his eyes. "Of course. But going slightly—very, very slightly—off the beaten track and focusing on the festival's origins might hit with the younger audience looking for experiences. It's not just colors and parades; it's a spiritual practice."

Rani considered it. "I don't know if I can sell it for the

paper edition, but it would be a great interactive piece online. Have you considered that?"

Sean groaned internally. He hated doing interactive shit. He was a photographer, not a multimedia presenter. Sean didn't know shit about power points and embedded... anything. "I think it's better for print. The colors alone—"

"Take the new girl."

Sean blinked. "What?"

"You can take the new girl." Rani glanced at him and reached for a different file. "Aubrey was eager to get her working, so she sent me her resume, it lists website building as part of her experience. Apparently, she used to do these fancy interactive presentations for people's weddings as part of the package."

Sean frowned. "Wait, she was a wedding photographer?"

Rani nodded. "Aubrey's daughter got married a couple weeks ago. This girl was the assistant to the guy who did her pictures."

"I'm trying not to be offended that she didn't ask me."

A laugh burst from his boss's mouth. "You? Do a wedding?"

"Every photographer does weddings at some point if they need to make money. They're hard work, but they pay the bills."

And this girl *starting* in weddings meant she definitely wasn't a trust fund kid. No one photographed weddings for fun. They were a shit-ton of work, and brides always underestimated the cost.

"Well, apparently, this girl impressed Aubrey enough that she offered her a job as an assistant, so boom." She smiled at him. "Congratulations, you have an assistant for this." She raised her hands and waved them. "Yay."

"I don't need an assistant."

"She's working for pennies and airfare, Sean. Give the girl a chance."

"What's that going to do to the budget?"

Rani shrugged. "I can figure out the budget. You think you can get one of your fancy celebrity friends on board?"

Sean didn't have many fancy celebrity friends, but he knew a lot of people who knew other people. "Would a social media celebrity work?"

"For an online piece, yes." She shuffled all the images, scraps of paper, and other research Sean collected and put them back in the manilla folder. "You know, if you knew how to put together a PowerPoint—"

"Oh fuck off."

She laughed, which was why she was one of Sean's favorite people. "Take the new girl. Hire some local talent for logistics. I'll get you a healthy budget. I have contacts in Delhi if you need them."

"They're probably the same contacts I have, but I'll let you know if my guys don't work out." He grabbed the folder from her. "I don't need an assistant."

"Work with the girl." Rani waved her hands. "Teach her your magic. Please don't teach her your charming personality; one of you is more than enough."

"I'm a fucking delight." He finished his coffee and stood up. "And I already made reservations for a nice hotel."

"Nice by whose standards?"

He smiled at her. "We work for a luxury magazine, Rani. They can foot the bill."

"JUNIPER HAWKINS?"

Juni looked up from a form that was asking about a life insurance beneficiary. "Do I have to have a life insurance beneficiary? How dangerous is this job?"

The woman calling her name smiled at her. "It's not, but apparently Aubrey is putting you on salary, which means you get benefits from the corporation. One of those benefits is a retirement account and a life insurance policy."

"Holy shit." She pressed her lips together. "Sorry, I shouldn't have said holy shit." She swallowed. "Twice. Uh, I'm Juni." She stuck out her hand. "Juniper is my legal name, but everyone calls me Juni."

"Juni, I'm Rani." They shook hands. "It's nice to meet you. I'm an editor here at Distinction. I coordinate all our staff photographers and take care of assignments."

"Oh wow." Juni jumped to her feet. "So you're like... my boss?"

Rani smiled. "I will be your supervisor, yes. And the life insurance policy is not big, but you do need to finish filling out all those forms." She motioned across the massive room filled with desks, computers, and bustling people. "Would you like to join me in my office? I have some time right now, and I can answer any questions you might have about the job or the forms."

"That would be awesome." Juni grabbed her backpack and slung it over her shoulder. "Do you think I need a brief-case if I work here?"

Rani was older than Juni, probably mid-thirties at least, and she was wearing what Juni was beginning to think of as the Distinction uniform. A super-hot and very expensive-looking outfit that was styled to look like it was thrown together but probably took two hours to compose.

Her new boss glanced over her shoulder. "Absolutely not. In fact, I'm going to suggest you do a regular streetwear feature for the online edition of the fashion division. Did you pick out your outfit?"

Juni glanced down at her second-hand store outfit. "Uh, yeah." It was cheap, and Juni hated looking like other people.

"You have a great eye. You're that cool girl that forward-thinking designers want to emulate. So no." Rani opened a glass door that led into a glass-walled office. "Do not change your wardrobe."

"Okay." She looked around, wondering where to sit. "So about the life insurance thing—"

"Complicated family?" Rani walked around to a chair on the other side of a long table with stacks of papers, files, and photographs organized in neat piles.

"Yeah." Juni sat on the other side of the table and sat her backpack on another chair. "You could say that."

"Your life insurance beneficiary does not have to be a relative, okay? And it's really not a huge amount, but it does go up for every year you work here. The magazine's owner is from France, so he has very different ideas about how employees should be paid."

Juni whispered. "Is that why I'm making so much?"

Rani's eyebrows went up. "I have no idea what they're paying you to start so—"

"Like, over three thousand dollars. A month." Juni still couldn't believe it. "And benefits."

"And travel." Rani smiled. "I promise you, that is standard for a starting photographer's assistant for the magazine. You will go up in salary if you continue to work here."

"Whoa." Juni sat back. "And Aubrey—Ms. Jackson, I mean, said that I can still do weddings on the weekends?"

"That shouldn't be a problem if you want to continue doing that. Most of our staff photographers also do private commissions. You may find that working here allows you to charge more for your services."

"No way." Juni smiled. "Can I tell you how weird I am?" She started filling out the forms again, listing her best friend Lauren as the person to get her life insurance if she fell off a ladder or something at work. "My mom is a mess, right? Married like three times. Well, technically, twice because she didn't officially marry the second one, but they had a traditional ceremony in Albuquerque. Then there was my dad, and they're miserable, but they refuse to get divorced for some reason, so it's not like I have a particularly healthy view of relationships or anything." She glanced up. "Are you married?"

Rani held up a ring with a truly massive emerald. "I just got married last year."

"Holy shit, that ring is gorgeous." Juni turned back to the forms. "Anyway, I don't even know if I believe in marriage as an institution for myself. Like, I would probably suck at it so hard, but I just fucking love *love*, you know?" She looked up, and Rani was looking...

Juni didn't know exactly because she barely knew the woman, but it didn't look hostile.

"So I did this wedding a couple months ago for an older couple who were gay, and they'd been together for like fifty years—can you believe that? But you know they never got married before because it was illegal. But I have a friend who was working with one of them—he's a theater manager downtown—and so they wanted to finally get married legally for their fiftieth anniversary and have this big party, so I offered to completely do that for free because how could I not, right?" Juni looked up, and Rani still wasn't talking, so she kept going. "I mean, I don't even care if they could have paid me. It was so fun and so inspiring, and the food was fucking amazing because one of them was Greek, and their kids cooked all the food, and that was the most lamb I have ever eaten before in my life." She blinked. "You're not vegetarian, are you? Or vegan?"

Rani was smiling ear to ear. "I'm not."

"Sorry, I can talk a lot sometimes." She set her pen and the clipboard on the table. "I'm finished with the forms."

"Did you tell that story to Aubrey when you met her?"

"I think so? I mean, we got to chatting, and Doug says I'm not supposed to talk with guests, but she kind of struck up the conversation because she was asking about my clothes, and we got to talking, and she's super nice." Juni rocked in her chair a little. "I promise I'm not usually this weird; I'm just kind of nervous."

"I don't think you're weird. I think you're very bright." Rani reached across and grabbed the clipboard. "And I suspect you're very talented."

"But you're definitely wondering why Aubrey hired me, right?"

Rani's eyes were kind. "No. I don't wonder that at all."

"Cool." What was she supposed to do now? What did a

staff photographer do to earn *three thousand dollars a month* in pay?

"Juni?"

She smiled. "Yes?"

"How would you like to go to India next month to cover the Holi festival with one of our senior photographers?"

"Do I have to pay for a plane ticket and a hotel and everything?"

"No, we pay for all of that."

"Oh my God, that is amazing."

two
unexpected
mathura

Delhi, India

"MADHU!" Sean waved when he spotted his old friend at the back of the crowded mass of drivers waiting outside the airport in Delhi. He turned to Juni and their celebrity guest for the week, Nami Hoffman, or Nami the Yogini as she was known on social media. "I see him."

Holi was only three days away, and the streets of the capital were already teeming with tourists, both foreign and domestic. Traffic was cacophonous, and shouts from hired drivers competed with blaring honks from the streets and the whining zip of motorbikes that cut through crowds and traffic.

"Oh. My god." Nami's manager and boyfriend, Devon, was carrying most of Nami's luggage, along with his own. "How... I mean, can we get through this?"

Nami laughed and turned to him. "Keep up, babe! Sean's got this."

Sean did "have this," but he kept glancing back to make sure Juni did as well. The girl was struggling behind him, carrying two large rolling bags full of equipment. He reached back to take one. "Come on. Stay with us."

"Trying."

Delhi could be a lot, even for experienced travelers.

"Don't worry." He gave her a reassuring smile. "We're going to a smaller city as soon as we get in Madhu's van."

"Mathura, right?"

"It's about three hours away."

She nodded, but her dark brown eyes darted around the crowds. She had olive skin and thick, straight hair he suspected was a natural brown, but she stuck out more than the rest of them by virtue of her evident nerves.

Sean had been to India numerous times and was used to the crowds and the press of bodies in public spaces. Nami was born in Mumbai and raised in California; he knew she traveled frequently. But a quick glance at Juni's passport while they were going through immigration showed a shiny blue cover and zero stamps. It was her first time out of the country, and Sean was bracing for culture shock.

"Hey!" Nami was waving at Madhu. "He's my cousin!" she shouted at the persistent drivers crowding around her and Devon. "We're meeting my cousin."

The taxi drivers lost interest and allowed them to pass through the crowd, redirecting their attention to other tourists who were making their way out of the airport.

"Is that guy really Nami's cousin?"

Sean glanced at Juni. "Who? Madhu?"

"Yeah."

"No, she just says that to get them to back off."

"Oh, right." Juni had slung her backpack to the front of her body like a baby carrier.

"You kept your wallet and everything in your backpack?"

She nodded. "Pickpockets?"

"Yep."

Sean craned his neck and saw Madhu shepherding Nami and Devon to a clearing in the crowd near the curb. He had already grabbed some of their bags and was chatting with his usual jovial enthusiasm.

"Madhu is a pro," Sean said. "I always call him when I'm in this part of the country. He and his brother will have all the details arranged."

He shot a cutting glance to an opportunistic pickpocket who sidled up to Juni. The boy caught Sean's knowing expression, flashed a grin, and darted back into the crowd.

"Sean!" Madhu waved again and pushed through the press of people meeting travelers, his massive frame making smaller men step aside as he approached them. "And who is your friend?"

"Let's get to the car, then I'll do introductions."

"Of course." Madhu ushered them to a clear spot on the sidewalk where Nami and Devon were waiting next to a tall man who watched the crowds with a glowering expression. "He's my brother-in-law," Madhu muttered to Sean. "I told him I was meeting a group from a US magazine, and he insisted on coming." The man shrugged. "I thought you might be able to pay him something for security."

The man standing next to Nami and Devon had to have been six and a half feet tall with shoulders bigger than barrel-chested Madhu and a glower that was steering the crowds away without saying a word.

Sean nodded. "I think I can work that into the budget." He slapped Madhu on the shoulder. "Where's Anuj?"

"Bringing the van around." He pointed his chin toward the corner. "Ah, I see him."

The black van pulled up to the curb where Nami and Devon were waiting, and the giant brother-in-law slid the door open for their guests of honor.

Sean, Juni, and Madhu started loading the bags in the back.

"Miss, miss." Madhu took the bags from Juni. "Please, let me. Make yourself comfortable in the van."

Juni's expression was grateful. "Thank you so much."

Madhu looked at Sean, who was staring at her departing back. "What is wrong with you?" Madhu elbowed him. "That girl is no bigger than my Preeti, and she's barely fifteen. Why were you letting her carry all this luggage?"

"Because she's a grown woman, and she offered. Juni is supposed to be my assistant," he said. "I'm letting her *assist*."

Madhu muttered something under his breath. "I will never understand American men."

"I didn't want her to come in the first place." He loaded the box with his lenses on top of the suitcases. "She's never even been out of the country."

"So you bring her to the most beautiful country in the world and make her carry her weight in suitcases?" Madhu shook his head. "We will talk later. Where are you staying?"

"Lalita Grand. I got a room for you and Anuj too." He glanced at their guard. "I didn't know about the brother-in-law."

Madhu slapped him on the shoulder. "You're taking two foreign women through the streets during Holi and trying to shoot pictures, my friend. You will be glad we have Umesh with us when we're in the middle of the chaos. He can sleep on the floor."

Mathura, India

THEY WERE PERCHED on a rooftop in Mathura, and Juni was holding a bounce board to reflect the sunset on Nami, who was posing an artful headstand as the fading light of Holi set over the streets of the old city. Sean Quinn was taking pictures of her in various positions, and they were almost out of sunlight.

All of them, from Madhu, the jovial, to Anuj, the silent giant named Umesh, was covered from head to toe in colored paint powder stuck to every crevice of their bodies after an entire day of walking through the narrow city streets of Mathura during one of the biggest holidays on the calendar.

"Can you give me one more minute?" Sean asked.

"Sure." Nami seemed genuinely meditative as she held the pose, her third on the rooftop, while her boyfriend-assistant-publicist checked her phone and took some quick snaps.

"Devon, you better not be posting those online." Sean didn't look away from his camera as he changed positions.

Juni shifted with him, knowing the light that he wanted to capture.

"I got the email from your editor," the man said.

The whitewashed and red-painted buildings that soared around them on the rooftop terrace bounced light in fascinating ways, and Juni watched intently as Sean used the narrow angle of the sunset and the reflectors Anuj had carted up to the roof to capture the slim woman in various yoga poses. Nami had offered to perch on the edge of the building, but Sean quickly nixed the idea.

She was a multicolored candle lit by the fading light. The team had brought Nami's hair supplies to the roof so she'd been able to smooth her dark brown hair back into a twist, then the makeup artist artfully dotted more paint in her tamed hair to match the riotous colors that covered her body.

"Juni, good work," Sean muttered.

Thank you. She didn't say it because she didn't want to distract him. The day had been exhausting, but they'd captured tons of footage, from the lazy breakfast on the edge of the river to a walk through the old city streets of Mathura.

Juni had never experienced anything like it in her life.

Music blasted through the city, and men, women, and children everywhere danced and ran through the streets, throwing paint at each other, tossing buckets of water on everyone who passed, and jumping on motorcycle taxis to zip across the city.

With four foreigners in their party—two of them

women—they'd been a visible target of the boys in the city, who took particular delight in drenching Nami and Juni if they even came close. At more than one point, the giant Umesh had to step in and bark a sharp reprimand to keep the boys from crowding the women.

There was no concept of personal space, and the crowds threatened to make Juni's desert heart seize.

She had no idea how to deal with so many people doing so many things and having no personal boundaries. She had grown up with silence, reserved handshakes, and open space. She was almost near her breaking point when Madhu finally led them into the private house that overlooked the old city with a giant balcony where Nami and Sean would finally get the shots that would complete the shoot for that day.

"Break." Sean snapped at the crew. "Get water. Nami, you're golden. Take it easy for a while."

The graceful woman gently folded herself in half as she came out of the headstand and reached for the water Devon was quick to hold out. "That was good."

"Fuck yes, that was good," Sean said. "I'm good, and you are too." He glanced at Juni. "Good instincts."

She gave him a slight nod and pretended that she wasn't dancing up and down inside. "Thanks."

The owner of the house, an older woman wearing a bright orange sari that was also covered with paint, walked out to the rooftop with a tray of drinks and plates of colorful snacks.

Juni tried not to stuff her face with the food, but it was difficult. Not only was she famished after nearly eight hours of straight work, but she was also entranced by the food they'd encountered in India.

Fruit on every corner, spicy fried treats, and rich curries. She hadn't grown up eating food that wasn't American, Mexican, or Navajo. Even in California, she'd been slow and cautious about trying new things. But in India? She'd had no choice but to try everything, and she was in love.

With the food.

She glanced at Sean, then looked away. He was showing Nami the camera, and the woman was nodding enthusiastically, a dimple showing on her cheek.

It was fine. That was cool. She hadn't expected him to show her first; that would have been presumptuous. Nami was the star of the shoot, the Indian-American influencer experiencing Holi in her birth country. They'd taken video, iPhone shots with lower resolution, and thousands of setting shots. It would be Juni's job when Sean was finished editing them to shape them into an online multimedia article with Sean's copy and photographs.

"Juni." He waved her over. "Nami wanted to know more about the interactive thing you and Rani are planning for the feature." He scooted over on the narrow couch. "Want to fill her in?"

Juni smiled. "Yeah! Of course." She took a seat and focused on Rani, not the fact that her head barely inched over Sean Quinn's shoulder. Did he really have to be that tall? "As I'm sure you know, most people under the age of thirty access news via their phones, right? So the idea is to create more than just a magazine posted online, but a multimedia story that kind of morphs from one picture to another as readers scroll down and engage the senses."

Nami nodded thoughtfully. "That's really dynamic. I like it."

"The vibe I'm aiming for is you taking readers on a tour of the festival with you. We got a lot of video following you through the city, so we can intersperse that with some of Sean's overhead shots—"

"Overhead?" He was frowning. "What are you talking about?"

"Uh, that you're like a foot taller than everyone else here except Umesh, so the angle looks like it's from overhead?"

The line of his mouth went flat. "I'm not that tall."

"You kind of are, but I'm sure in Scandinavia, you'd blend in fine." She turned back to Nami. "Okay, so it's going to be movement, visuals sliding in from the side, almost like people coming at you on the street. It's going to be really amazing. I promise."

"I love this." Nami's eyes lit up.

"And we can incorporate music and audio with it as well. I've been taking recordings of ambient noise all day; we can intersperse that with licensed music, and then we can slow it down at the end of the article." Juni gestured to the rooftop where they were sitting. "Bring in that meditative quality. Slower music, softer colors."

Sean broke in. "And that's where my writing can really get deeper and focus on the spiritual roots of the festival and the city. Draw people in to visit Mathura for the history, the experience, the spiritual practice." He reached for another fried goodie. "And the food, of course."

Nami looked at Juni. "Some of the best food in India. I'm telling you. Right here." The woman's face was glowing beneath all the colorful paint. "I love this. And I'm super flattered that you wanted to include me." She looked between Sean and Juni. "You know, the two of you make an outstanding team."

Sean almost choked on his food, but he covered it up with a cough.

Juni looked at him, then quickly looked away. "Thanks."

three
chiang mai temptation

Chiang Mai, Thailand

IT WAS one thing for Rani to force Sean to babysit the new girl on a trip to India for an online feature, but when Juniper Hawkins showed up in Chiang Mai just before Songkran, he was more than a little confused.

"Juni?" Sean froze in the lobby of his hotel near the night market in Chiang Mai. He'd been sent to cover the New Year's festival, Songkran, and he wasn't counting on company.

But when he walked downstairs, there she was. There was not a single place in the world Sean wouldn't recognize that pink-streaked head and pert chin.

She looked up, and she was wearing heart-shaped sunglasses and a smile. "Hey."

Rani hadn't told him. Of course, she hadn't. Juni had quickly become a darling of the fashion division and, over the past year, had filled her once-empty passport with Shanghai, Goa, Sydney, Nairobi, and Singapore, not to mention a few other places he probably hadn't heard of. He rarely saw her in the LA offices, and he'd only met her in passing once when they happened to be flying out of LAX at the same time. They'd had a drink, and then he hadn't seen her for another three months.

"I didn't know you were coming to Chiang Mai." He hiked his black backpack higher on his shoulder. "Rani sent you?"

"Yes." She jumped to her feet. "I was actually in Bangkok to do a street-style feature, and she told me you were going to be up here and suggested I come up to do another interactive." She stretched her arms over her head, and a hint of a tanned belly peeked out. "Looking a little rough there, Spider."

"Please don't call me that."

Juni put a finger to her temple. "But the image of you bracing yourself halfway up an alleyway in Mathura will never leave my mind." She was wearing a bright orange tank top and a pair of multicolored loose pants she had probably bought in the market. "Sorry. You wear all black and climb walls, you're going to get a nickname like Spider."

The Holi feature with Nami garnered a massive surge of traffic to the website and cemented Juni as the new Bright Young Thing on staff. It probably helped that she always had a smile, worked her ass off, and was exceptionally talented.

Sean had spent the previous week alone in a monastery on the Myanmar border with no one who spoke English and only his very rudimentary Thai. He'd shifted into snake form halfway through the week and spent days exploring the forest before he returned to the very confused monks.

As much as he appreciated the respite time in animal form, he'd never been happier to see a familiar face.

"Wait." She cocked her head and narrowed her eyes. "Was that... I mean, I might be imagining it."

The corner of his mouth inched up as he tried to suppress his smile. "You're obnoxious."

"It's true." Her eyes went wide. "Sean Quinn is happy to see me!" She raised both her arms like she was calling a football match. "Score! He *can* be friendly."

"I'm going to make you fill out both our expense reports."

"Boo!" She bumped his shoulder. "Hiss. Do not like. What's the plan for today?"

He kept walking out of the lobby, knowing she would follow. "The plan is to go out while it's still relatively calm and get some street shots. Are we doing an interactive?"

"That's the plan." Sean glanced down at her.

"Stan."

He frowned. "Who's Stan?"

"That's the plan, Stan." She shook her head. "You really need to keep up with the kids' lingo, old man."

He barely kept from laughing. "I don't think anyone over the age of twelve says that."

She shoved her heart-shaped sunglasses up her nose. "You poor, out-of-touch geezer."

"Whatever." She was a fucking delight, and he hated admitting it. "So we're doing an interactive. Did you bring a recorder?"

"I did." Juni didn't walk behind him anymore. She had her familiar old tie-dyed backpack on her back and scrappy sandals with gold-painted toenails.

"Good. You look like a tourist, so just hang around and record the music and the crowd noises while I get some broader shots before the water really gets going."

"Oh, right." She pulled a recorder from her pocket and looked at it. "This is not waterproof."

"Which is why we're going out this early and why Rani sprang for the balcony room in the middle of town."

Her mouth dropped open. "Your room has a balcony?"

"How else are we supposed to get photos of this parade when everyone is throwing buckets of water at anything that moves?"

"Good point." Her eyes were moving back and forth as they walked toward the center of town. "Thai people are basically the friendliest ever, right? Everyone was so nice in Bangkok. I was tempted to rent an apartment there. Do you know how much apartments are? So much cheaper than LA."

Sean pulled out his camera and started taking pictures as they walked. He had a hard time imagining anyone who wouldn't be charmed by Juni and her enthusiasm for literally everything in life. "There are a few photographers on staff who have places in Asia. It makes sense if you spend a lot of time here."

Juni moving to Asia produced an unexpected twist in his chest, and he didn't know why. It wasn't as if he saw her in the office regularly. They didn't have any mutual friends.

You don't have any friends in LA.

Maybe the reason he was spending more and more time as a snake these days was he needed to get back to the Springs. It had been years since he'd done anything more than sneak into town in the dead of night, drink the water from the spring, and hightail it out of that desert wasteland before anyone in his family saw him.

Seeing Juni reminded him of home.

He kept snapping pictures. "You been home recently?"

"To Albuquerque?" The smile fell from her face. "Why?"

"You said you had a brother there."

She was quiet, focusing on fiddling with the controls of the sound recorder. "It's complicated."

He stared at the top of her head, cursing himself for bringing up something that had stolen the light from her eyes. "I get it."

She looked up and met his gaze. Then she nodded and went back to adjusting the settings on her recorder.

FUCKING SEAN QUINN. She'd been able to travel for a year, working at her dream job, and she hadn't thought about her family in all that time.

One mention of home from him?

And she was right back there.

She was sitting in the corner of the stone balcony in his room, grabbing crowd shots of the revelry as Sean used a larger lens from the other corner to get closeups as the party continued.

"The light is so good right now."

The parade was moving slowly through the street, water flying and spattering in mid-air, catching the light and scattering rainbows everywhere. Music was loud, laughter was louder.

They'd been taking pictures for five hours, and the festival showed no signs of slowing down.

Juni was deep in concentration, recording a group of boys with water balloons, when she felt a stream of icy water hit her leg.

She looked up with a gasp to see Sean holding a neon green water pistol.

"Oops." He was grinning.

It was so out of character for him she almost didn't speak. "Did you... just squirt gun me?"

He raised his eyebrows and looked at the plastic gun in his hand. "No. A rogue macaque parachuted onto the balcony, shot you, then shoved this in my hand."

She frowned. "Who are you?"

Sean laughed, and the smile on his face made his eyes crinkle in the corners a little bit. He was older, but not that much older, even though most of the time, he was the wicked serious professional anytime he was around her.

"Come on." He hopped off the balcony and reached for her hand. "We've been working all day. Don't you want to go wander around?"

She looked down at her orange shirt and brightly colored pants. Water wouldn't ruin them. "Sure." She shrugged. "Why not? Can we get some food?"

"Have you tried the crispy tofu noodles yet?"

"No."

"Put the camera away; we're going out." He walked to his bed and carefully stowed his equipment while Juni scanned the mystery of his bedroom.

"Rani said you've been in Thailand for a few weeks."

She carefully put her lenses into neat storage units and zipped them up. "No souvenirs?"

"I was in a monastery north of Chiang Rai," he said. "Not too much shopping."

"Oh, right." A monastery? When she pictured Sean Quinn on his own, he was having a cocktail at a cool party with important people or maybe partying at a new club where he ignored the women to make them want him.

It was not him meditating with monks. "Are you... Buddhist?"

He smirked. "Catholic with maybe a little Buddhist mixed in. I like the quiet."

"Cool." Juni was raised with pretty much nothing. Her older half-brother had spent a lot of time with her mother's brother on the Navajo reservation where they were from, but by the time Juni came around, her mother was pretty disconnected from her culture.

Probably because of her dad.

Probably because of a lot of things.

"Okay, we should definitely go out." Sean turned around. "Give me a second." He pulled the black t-shirt over his head and grabbed a white t-shirt from his backpack.

Juni hadn't expected tattoos. Or the muscles.

She turned and faced the balcony, trying to understand why the sight of Sean Quinn's naked back elicited a blush from a girl who was far from virginal.

She cleared her throat. "So, did you get your work done here in Thailand?"

"The tattoos? Some. Some back in LA. I'm done."

She turned around, and he was smirking.

Juni raised an eyebrow. "What?"

"Did I offend your modest sensibilities?" He stuffed the black shirt in his backpack. "Sorry. You've been on fashion shoots."

There was no modesty on most shoots where models regularly disrobed.

"I..." She didn't know what to say. "Do you work out?"

He smiled again. "No. But I climb a lot of trees in my spare time."

"See? Spider."

He stuck the bright green water gun in the waistband of his black jeans. "You ready?"

"Let's hit the streets, Quinn."

SONGKRAN WAS IN FULL SWING, and they were only steps out of the hotel lobby when two little boys ran up and water-bombed them with shrieks of laughter. Sean pulled Juni in front of him and used her as a shield, aiming a stream of water at the boys with Juni in the crossfire.

"What was that?" Laughter burst from her mouth, and there were butterflies in her chest.

"What?" He grabbed her hand and pulled her into the crowd. "Keep up, Hawkins."

They became part of the moving mass of humanity celebrating the new year festival with buckets, water guns, and hoses dragged from every storefront and house. Everyone from the young to the old was out and celebrating. There were even a few white-haired seniors flinging cups of water from narrow balconies over the streets.

Juni was from the southwestern US. Water was a

precious resource to be saved, conserved, and rationed. The lushness of the city, the fountains, and the showers of water felt like the most indulgent celebration she could imagine.

Flowers dripped from trees, and water ran in rivulets down the street and over her body as first her shirt, then her hair, then everything she was wearing became soaked in the celebration.

It was rich in a way that she could never put into words, and she almost reached for her camera before she realized she'd left everything but her keys and some cash back at the hotel.

"Don't think about your camera," Sean shouted over the blast of music in the streets. "Just be here. Take everything in."

Sean wove their hands together and pressed her arm to his side, keeping her close as he navigated the crowds.

Juni took the gift of his attention, the showers, the roar of humanity, and she let it wash over her like the water.

Sean checked on her as they pushed through the crowd. "You okay? You having fun?"

"This is amazing!" She raised her other arm when a little white-haired woman on a roof balcony waved at her.

The old woman took a tin cup of water and flung it in Juni's direction, hitting the side of Sean's head in the process.

Juni burst into laughter, and so did the old woman. She flung her arm around Sean's neck and laughed into his shoulder. "I'm sorry, but the look on your face!"

Sean smiled and shouted something to the woman, and she waved and kept laughing.

Juni looked up. "What did you say to her?"

"I told her thank you for the shower." He brushed a sopping wet strand of hair from her eyes, his fingers lingering at her temple.

He blinked and looked away as Juni let go of his neck. "We should keep going."

"Yes!" Juni shoved out a breath over her racing heart. "Where to next?"

He looked over the crowd; his height gave him an advantage. "Let's head to the university."

She had no idea where she was going, so she was glad that he kept her hand firmly in his. She was pressed up against him in the crowd, their bodies bumping together as they made their way through the streets.

Women threw flowers from rooftops, the bright yellow and pink petals clinging to her soaked clothes and hair.

The revelry reached a fever pitch in front of the Three Kings monument, where a band was playing on a water-protected stage, and speakers blasted the music all over the square.

Vendors shouted from the shops and from rolling carts, hawking water guns and buckets. Hoses were connected end to end until they stretched into the square, leaving pools of water for revelers to fill their buckets or their toys.

The crowd was dancing to the music, and Sean pressed toward it, keeping Juni with him. They were far from the only foreigners in the celebration. Faces from all over the world joined the Thai smiles, and the mood was electric.

He turned when they reached the bandstand and put his arms at her waist, guiding her into the rhythm of the pop band playing on the stage. He slid his hand to the small of her back and moved.

God, he had rhythm.

Juni felt his thighs pressing against hers and their bodies moving together. She looked up and saw him staring at her. His lips were parted, and water dripped from his soaking wet hair onto his forehead and down angled cheekbones.

He put warm hands on her cheeks, leaned down, and pressed his lips to hers.

The contact was electric, and he stole her breath.

Whoa.

Wow.

He pulled back. "That was stupid."

"Probably." She reached up and drew him down to kiss her again.

Their mouths met over and over as the world spun around them. Sean's kiss was firm and knowing, his large hands holding her face like she was something precious and rare. Water and flower petals whipped through the air, and everything was magic.

four
awkwardness
in fez

Fez, Morocco

SEAN FROZE when Rani said the name. "Wait, who?"

"I'm sending Juni," Rani said. "She's in Spain for a fashion thing; it's convenient. Please don't argue with me."

"I..." Sean struggled. It had been nearly a year since Chiang Mai. He'd spent most of it hopping from one place in Europe to the next, taking whatever assignments Rani threw at him, pissing off the staff in New York and London by being so available.

And avoiding Juniper Hawkins.

He tugged at his hair. "I'm not arguing about you sending Juni; I just wish you'd given me a little more notice before I—" Someone knocked at his door. "Shit."

"That's probably her. I gave her your hotel name, and you know she can get anyone to tell her anything."

"Yeah." He remembered. "I know."

"Just be nice. Every time you work together, it's magic. Just suck up whatever personal problem you have with her and deal." Rani huffed out a breath. "I know you think she's young, and yes, I agree she is on paper, but let's just say she's had a lot of life thrown at her at a young age, okay?"

"Fine." He knew all that. "I'll be nice." He walked to the door and opened it to see Juni standing on the other side with an amused smirk.

Rani was still talking. "Your work in the South of France was stellar, by the way."

She looked exactly the same but better. She was tan, and she'd exchanged the pink streaks in her hair for gold. She was wearing a bright green skirt and some kind of white top that wrapped around her body and left nothing to the imagination, all while covering every inch of her skin.

"Thank you, Rani. I have to go." He opened the door wide, and Juni sauntered into his room. "Bye."

"Say hi to Juni."

Sean hung up the call and gripped the phone in his right hand. "Hey."

Juni was already making herself at home in the hammock chair mounted to the ceiling in his suite, kicking her leg out as she swung back and forth. He wanted to throw her on the bed and fuck her. He also wanted to kiss her for days.

She knew it. She had to know.

The corner of her mouth turned up. "Hi, stranger."

He lifted the phone. "Rani says hi."

"Hi back. I was in Madrid this morning."

He stuck his phone in his pocket. "And now you're here."

She raised both eyebrows. "And you don't look happy

to see me, Spider! What's up with that? I can't be the first girl you ghosted after a date."

What they'd had in Chiang Mai wasn't a date; it was bad judgment and his dick thinking for him. Unfortunately, he hadn't been able to get her off his mind since.

Sean leaned against the wall all the way across the room. "That wasn't a date. That was me being impulsive and lonely."

"Ouch." She didn't look offended. She still had that amused little smirk on her fucking adorable, kissable pixie face. "So, any warm body would have done?"

"Don't insult both of us like that."

"Oh, I'm not insulted." She smiled. "If anything, I'm *flattered*. Who knew one afternoon of kissing me in Thailand could make Sean Quinn run that far from home?"

He kicked off the wall, impossibly drawn to whatever inner fire illuminated this woman-girl-fairy. He may have been a shapeshifter, but he was dead certain Juni had some kind of magic because she'd been reading his mind.

He crouched down in front of the hammock chair. "It was a moment. I will admit it was beautiful and memorable. I was caught up in the energy of the day. Can we leave it at that and be professionals?"

She leaned forward and rested her elbows on her knees, her chin resting on her fist. "We can't even be friends?"

Friends was a loaded word for Sean, not unlike family. He had work colleagues, he had peers, he had co-workers and fellow professionals.

He counted very few people as friends.

"What about friendly professionals?" he asked.

Juni rolled her eyes. "Are you always like this?"

"I like to be specific." He liked assurances too, but life wasn't keen on allowing those to the bastard son of an outcast clan.

"You can call me a friendly professional, Spider." She brushed a strand of hair off his forehead. "But I'm going to call you a friend because I don't have many of them, and I've kind of been working on collecting a few more."

Damn her for being bright and honest and beautiful and right in front of him but completely out of reach.

Despite the emotions churning in his brain, he couldn't keep the corner of his mouth from turning up. "I've met a lot of weird people in my life, but I've never met anyone like you."

"I'm going to take that as a compliment." She batted her eyelashes. "I'm one of a kind, Quinn." She flung herself back in the hammock chair, and he tried not to notice the curve of her waist where her shirt inched up. "Why do you always get the best hotel rooms? This one has a balcony too."

He sprung for extra so he wouldn't be closed in by four walls, which was something he was slightly manic about. As far as he knew, most shifters from Cambio Springs were the same. "It's because I'm old, and I've been doing this for a lot of years."

"You're not that old."

I feel that old.

He nudged the swing chair with his foot and watched her swing back and forth. For a second, he indulged his mind and imagined her naked, legs spread, with her head thrown back in this exact chair, while he kneeled in front of her and—

Nope.

Absolutely not.

"Come on." He needed to distract himself fast. "Let's go get you some food. Want to try a camel burger?"

"Not even a little bit."

"BALAK, BALAK!" Juni jumped out of the way as a donkey bearing two large bags of oranges trotted down the middle of the narrow street.

Her editor had promised two days for a speedy tour of "Evolving Fez," and those two days had passed in a whirl. She and Sean met their local crew the same afternoon she arrived and spent two days dodging shouts of "Balak, balak!" as donkeys and carts shuffled goods ranging from concrete bricks to Amazon packages through the narrow streets of the Medina.

They traced their way through the old city taking pictures and talking with shopkeepers, butchers, house-wives, and old men. Juni stuck to Sean, convinced that she'd become hopelessly lost in the tangled streets and squares of the old city.

"Balak, balak!" She pressed against a stone wall to avoid a hand cart speeding past her, her toes coming within inches of being crushed by a load of bright orange soda pop.

Juni looked up to see Sean pointing his camera straight at her.

"Nice," she said. "Did you catch my scared face?"

"You know, they do say that sugar can kill you, but I didn't realize they were being literal." He hung his DSLR from the strap around his neck and reached for her hand. "We're done."

"Done done?" She let out a breath and put her recorder away. "Did we get enough of the ambient—"

"Yeah, I think we're good. I let Fatima and Alfie go home. They invited us over for dinner later if you want to go."

"Home-cooked food or camel burgers?" She pretended to think. "I don't know; it's a tough one."

Their translator and her husband had been their links to the old city, as Fatima's father was a prominent shop-keeper, and she was a well-known guide. They'd had welcome and friendly faces everywhere they went.

"Dinner with them sounds good, but I want a shower first." She was pretty sure the smell of leather clung to her skin and hair.

"We'll head back to the hotel and clean up. Alfie said he'd come over about nine to pick us up for dinner." He held out his hand for a moment before he pulled it back. "I'm pretty sure I know the way back."

Poor baby. He couldn't even hold her hand without violating whatever strange moral code he'd constructed for himself.

"I'm following you, Quinn, so don't get us lost."

The first time she'd met him in India, she thought he was just antisocial, but she'd seen too much evidence other-wise firsthand and from mutual "friendly co-workers." He wasn't an asshole; he was generous with his time and often volunteered when there was a shit assignment no one else wanted.

He lived quietly, and according to something Rani let

slip once, he sent a good portion of his income back to family who were somewhere in the California desert. He had *not* had a privileged upbringing, of that Juni was sure.

After their day in Chiang Mai, she was pretty certain the man was lonely. Plain *lonely*. He lived in a world of constant movement and very few ties. He was well-regarded but not well-known.

They turned a corner, and she saw their hotel in the distance. "Nice work, Quinn."

"I have a good sense of direction."

She decided to poke him a bit. "Does it run in your family?"

He glanced at her. "You could say that."

Part of her wished that working with him was more difficult, so Rani wouldn't constantly be pushing the two of them together, but the problem was, they didn't just work well together; they complimented each other. Juni had done some of her best work with Sean Quinn.

It was annoying as shit.

She left him in the lobby. "Okay, I'm going to head up to my room and clean up. Maybe lay down a little. Just text me when Alfie gets here."

THREE HOURS LATER, Juni was lying on her bed in a kaftan she'd picked up in the market and a face mask she'd bought in Singapore, listening to music from Spain.

She was an international badass now. She still had to pinch herself at times. The little girl growing up in the South Valley had only dreamed of going to all the places

Juni had been. Reality was so much better than her imagination.

Someone knocked on her door. She glanced at her
phone and saw that it was only eight o'clock. Could Alfie
have shown up early?

She peeled the face mask off, rubbed the remaining
serum over her skin, and walked to the door, opening the
small window cut into the wood.

"Hey." Sean was bending down, peering through the
window. "Disaster."

She pulled the door open. "What happened?"

He grimaced. "A pipe broke in Fatima and Alfie's bathroom. They warned us it's a pretty bad scene over there."

"Oh no! That's awful."

"I know."

She widened the door to let him in. "Come in."

Sean walked in, but only a few feet. "Fatima has all this
food cooked, so she's sending it over with a friend, and the
friend is going to leave it at the front desk for us since she
promised us dinner."

"Oh my God, she's too sweet. That's so thoughtful
with all the chaos in her house."

"I know." He looked around. "Alfie said they'd come
over in the morning to meet us for tea before we catch our
flights, though."

"That's nice. I wouldn't want to leave the city without
saying thank you." She stared at him. "So...?"

"So." He pursed his lips. "I guess we're going to eat in
our rooms?"

"I hate eating alone." She scrunched up her nose. "I
vote we eat in your room. It's much nicer."

"Juni, I don't know if that's a good—"

"No nakedness allowed." She raised a hand. "I promise not to seduce you if you promise not to seduce me." She tried to keep a straight face. "It will be difficult, so we might need wine."

"Absolutely not." He laughed. "Okay, I'll text you when the food comes. Meet me downstairs, and we can eat on my balcony."

"Perfect!"

THE VIEW over the city was intoxicating, and so was the wine she'd brought and opened, despite his objections.

She reached over the table and grabbed his empty glass.

"Juni—"

"No." She raised a hand. "We're trying something new, friend."

"Okay... *friend*."

She looked up and winked at him. "I knew you'd give in eventually."

"What are we trying?"

She stared at the wine glasses so she didn't chicken out. "We're going to get drunk and honest, with no nakedness and no contact allowed, even if I do want to kiss you on this incredibly romantic balcony." She looked up, wine glass in hand, and froze when she saw what could only be considered a feral look in his eyes.

"Honest?"

She wanted to take it back, but she couldn't, so she plowed ahead with feigned bravado. "Yep." She shoved his glass at him. "I'm already pretty buzzed—clearly—so I'll go first. I think you're crazy attractive, and I'm not talking about your looks, even though those are pretty stellar."

He sat back and took a gulp of wine, but said nothing, so she plowed forward.

"I..." She laughed a little. "I got an apartment in Chiang Mai. Remember when we were talking about that? And I do spend a lot of time there because I'm in Asia for work a lot, and it's a great city to be based out of, and I love it. But *really*, I kept hoping that someone might tell you that I was there and you would show up." She raised her hands. "Ta-da! Suddenly. And I would see you, and you would see me, and you would know what it meant." She swallowed half her wine glass. "Dumb, right?"

"Not dumb." His voice was rough; he sounded like he'd been smoking. "I heard that you were living there, and I thought a hundred times about going and pretending to run into you."

She felt like someone had stabbed her in the heart and then shot sunshine straight into her veins. "Why didn't you?"

"Because I... can't." He swallowed hard. "And I'm not going to give you a sob story about how messed up my family is or why I never seem to be able to settle in one place or keep friends or even why I ghosted you for a year because there's no excuse for that." He swallowed the rest of his wine in one gulp. "I don't have a girlfriend, Juni. I don't have a wife, and I probably never will. I won't have kids if I can help it because I'm already responsible for a lot that aren't mine, and I've basically abandoned them, and I don't have an excuse for that either. Just know that when things get hard, I run away. That's what I do. That's what I'm good at."

She had wanted him to respond, but now his words were burning her ears. "Sean—"

"Juni, I want you so fucking much it's driving me crazy, and I wish to God you weren't so damn talented and bright and real because it only makes me want you more." He set his empty glass down on the table. Hard. "And I'm a bastard for saying that, aren't I?" He looked up and met her eyes. "You're so energetic and alive and fucking passionate about life. And I want it. I barely know you, but I *want* that."

She leaned forward. "And why don't you think I could under—?"

"I would take all that brightness and life, and I would just...." He shook his head. "I would suck the life out of you."

Juni sat back, watching the dark scowl on his face turn to despair.

He continued. "My situation, circumstances—whatever you want to call it—would suck the life out of you, and I would hate myself for fucking ever." He shook his head. "So I won't do it." He sniffed. "I refuse."

She sat back in her seat. He wasn't drunk, and that made it so much worse.

"I think you should go." Sean swallowed hard. "You should go."

Juni wanted to cry. She wanted to kiss his face and hold him and tell him it couldn't be that bad, but she'd known too many damaged families not to believe him. He wasn't lying. He believed every word he said.

"Do you want me to go?" Her voice sounded brittle to her own ears, like dried-up branches cracking in the wind.

"Nope." His smile was grim. "So you should definitely go."

Juni got up, walked to the door, and left.

SEAN DIDN'T MEET them for coffee in the morning.

five
maasai mara resignation

Nairobi, Kenya

THE NEXT TIME he saw her, Sean had accepted it. Nothing could ever happen between them. Nothing good enough for her.

But when Juni's eyes met his across the runway at Wilson Airport in Nairobi, and he saw she was waiting for the same flight, she smiled, and her eyes were kind.

He walked over and wrapped her in the biggest hug he could give her without cracking her ribs.

"Hey." She rubbed his back. "How you doing, friend?"

"It's good to see you." He kissed the top of her head. "How've you been?"

"Good." She kept her arm around his waist as they walked to a pair of empty chairs. "Is this another interactive?"

"Nope. She didn't email you?" He glanced at her hair. "I like the red."

"Thanks! And not really. She didn't have to. She knows I've been dying to do a safari shoot."

"You're not going to be disappointed, I promise."

She was nearly jumping up and down with excitement. "So what can I expect?"

"This is a feature for the big fall Africa edition—not going to lie, it's basically advertising for this company—but they're comping almost everything, so we're going to get the royal treatment."

She was quivering with excitement. "So what am I expecting here? Luxury hotel in the middle of the savannah? Bush camp?"

"It's a camp." He heard their flight number called and walked with Juni to the stairs leading to the prop plane that would take them to the Mara. "But it's not a bush camp. We're talking those giant old-fashioned canvas tents—"

"Like in old movies?"

"Absolutely. But they've hooked up a water system, so there are bathrooms, showers, bathtubs, all the modern amenities. I think there are even air conditioners, though I doubt we'll need them."

"Can I tell you?" She took a long breath before she ducked into the plane. "This dry air is giving me life."

He settled next to her in the passenger seats a few rows back from the pilot and made sure Juni sat by the window. "How's Chiang Mai?"

"Awesome. In retrospect, I'm so glad I rented there instead of Bangkok because as much as I love that city, it's even more hectic than LA."

"How often do you fly back?" The plane began to taxi as they settled in.

"Oh, I'm there every month or so. I still have the apartment in Venice with my friend Lauren, but she covers about two-thirds of it right now since her boyfriend is living there. Thank god we have this little old man who's our landlord and hasn't raised the rent."

"Oh, that's nice. You should really think about buying when you can, though. Even if you rent it out, it's worth it."

She elbowed him as the plane took off and soared over Nairobi. "Well, some of us aren't making the big bucks on European fashion shoots."

"You could if you wanted to."

She wrinkled her nose. "I'm doing fine. And Rani will comp my flights sometimes because it costs her less to fly me to assignments from Chiang Mai. How about you? Where have you been hiding?""

"Believe it or not, I was in Australia for about three months. Went for work and decided to use some vacation time after."

"Nice!" She sat up straight as the plane leveled out. "How was that? I feel like I would worry about snakes and spiders the entire time I was there."

"Oh yeah?" Sean barely kept from bursting into laughter. "You have a phobia about snakes or something?"

"Not a phobia, per se, but have you seen some of the snakes there?"

He nodded. "Believe it or not, I have."

"There's big snakes, and then there's *big snakes*." She shook her head. "I'm just not cool with that."

He bit his lip to keep from laughing. "So you're saying that you just can't handle that much snake?"

"Hey!" She pointed at him, and her eyes were dancing.

"I'm being good, Mr. Quinn. Do you see me making sexual innuendos? No, I am not." She turned to the window. "Please behave yourself."

"All I said is that you're clearly inexperienced with longer snakes. If you're making something sexual about that" —he covered the laugh with a cough— "I'm sorry, but that's on you." He shook his head. "Not my fault you have a dirty mind."

She bit her lip to keep from laughing. "You're terrible."

"I personally think snakes are friendly."

She glanced at his lap. "They can be very friendly if they want to be."

He pointed at her. "Ah! That's on you." He shook his head. "Dirty, dirty mind."

"MR. QUINN!" A young man wearing a deep green polo shirt greeted them when they landed on the dirt strip at the far end of their one-hour journey. "Miss Hawkins. I am so happy to meet you both." He stuck his hand out. "My name is Benjamin, and I'm the camp manager. Welcome to the Mara. We're so excited for you to see the camp."

"Thank you so much!" Juni shook his hand. "I don't know if you can tell, but I'm really excited to be here." She leaned closer. "It's my first time in Kenya."

"We welcome you." Benjamin turned to Sean. "And welcome back, Mr. Quinn. Thank you so much for accepting our invitation. We were thrilled when our site was chosen for the feature in Distinction."

Sean shook the man's hand. "Thank you. I'm really excited to be back."

"We have a full camp this week, so we were relieved when your editor assured us that the accommodations would be sufficient for you both." He picked up a bag one of the luggage crew handed to him with the safari company tag. "I assure you, the tent is more than adequate."

Sean blinked. "I'm sorry, what?"

Benjamin's eyes went wide. "I was assured that this would not be a problem, and when I saw you together, I thought I understood."

"Tent?" Juni cleared her throat. "Sorry, was that a singular *tent*? Not tents?"

"I did not think this would be an issue because your editor assured me that you worked together, and I assumed she had informed you." He looked from Sean to Juni. "I am sorry if there was a misunderstanding, but there is only one tent available right now."

Maasai Mara, Kenya

JUNI STOOD with her backpack on her back and her carry-on in her hand. A massive king-size bed strewn with white linens and flower petals dominated the center of the space.

"One tent, but two bedrooms." She looked up at Sean. "This is fine."

"No, it's not." He'd been irritable the entire ride from the airport. "I'm going to talk to the manager and see—"

"Nooooo, I don't want to be *those* people!" She squeezed his arm. "Do not talk to Benjamin. Leave it." She walked into the massive canvas tent that was pitched on the edge of the savannah, with acacia trees shading it and fresh flowers on the coffee table in the sitting area. "This place is huge."

She turned to the left and walked down a narrow canvas corridor that connected the main room with another smaller tent that held two smaller beds and another bathroom. "Sean, this is basically a tent house. We have plenty of room. I'll just take the kids' room."

"Absolutely not." He strode down the hallway and threw his bags on the bed. "This is your first time on safari, your first time in Kenya, and I always get the fancy room, remember? You take the king-size bed."

Juni laughed. "You're joking. Your feet are going to hang off the end."

"Please, you think this is the worst place I've slept?" He scoffed. "No rats in the ceiling, Juni. It's a palace."

Okay, so many questions, but as always with Sean, she knew she wouldn't get more to the story than that. She turned, eyeing the king bed that looked like a cloud. "Are you sure?" She narrowed her eyes and looked at his feet. "You're not going to be comfortable in here, and I'm tiny. I'm comfortable anywhere."

"I'm sure." He took her by the shoulders and guided her back to the main bedroom. "Put your stuff down, put your feet up..." He swept his arm out to the drawn-back door of the tent where long grass waved in the breeze and a pair of antelope trotted by. "...and enjoy your view."

She couldn't take her eyes away from the view. "This is so much better than a balcony."

Sean came to stand next to her. "It really, really is."

Juni put her arm around Sean's waist and leaned into him. "Thanks."

"Anytime." His voice was rough, and the arm he put around her shoulders hugged her tight.

Juni put her other arm around his waist and hugged him tight. His loneliness was vibrating like a live wire. "How long are we here?"

"Three nights, four days."

"Cool."

She wasn't really sure what love was, but Juni had a sneaking suspicion that she loved him. It was an inconvenient realization when she knew he was broken in a way she wasn't.

As hard as her childhood had been, she had never felt unloved. Overlooked? Yes. Ignored? Definitely. Saddled with far too much responsibility for her age? Sure. But she knew her dysfunctional, sad parents loved her, and she knew other people did too. Her half-brother Caleb. Her best friend Lauren and her family.

Sean was a gaping void of loneliness and guilt.

"Come on." She pulled him toward the massive king bed. "Just lay down and stretch out before dinner. Clothes on."

"Juni—"

"We're adults, and we're tired." She nudged him to sit. "Just relax and put your feet up. We've got three long days of work in front of us."

He took a deep breath, but he took off his shoes, laid down, and in moments, they were both asleep.

"STILL." His voice was in her ear, and he was so close she could feel his breath on her neck. "Oh my God, please tell me you have him in the frame."

"I have him in the frame." Her heart was racing.

"Don't move."

"Sean shut up." She had this, and she needed him to stop distracting her.

They were tracking a leopard that was crawling along the edge of the riverbank at dusk, stalking a herd of wildebeests as the animals waited to cross a river.

There was a pride of lionesses lurking at the crossing, so the herd had fallen back, and the leopard was taking advantage.

Sean had the camera on him, and Juni had the video.

It was pure luck that they'd found him at all. Their game spotter had spent three days trying to find a leopard for them. Not all that important to the magazine, but it was the last animal on Juni's mental checklist.

She'd spent three days in heaven, riding across the savannah, drinking cocktails around the campfire, and laughing with the other parties who were staying in the camp. All of them assumed that Sean and Juni were a couple, and they'd done nothing to dissuade them of the idea. Sean had been uncharacteristically affectionate once they'd woken up from their nap the first afternoon, as if the moment she'd taken nakedness off the table, he could relax.

"This footage is amazing." Juni was praying the footage turned out.

"These shots are good." He glanced at his display. "So good." He nodded at their driver. "Great position, Luke."

"You're lucky he's hungry tonight."

Juni was fascinated by the wily predator. She'd seen her share of lions, and they were stunningly beautiful, but the leopard was elusive, evasive, and very hard to spot, especially in the dark. There wasn't another animal she wanted to photograph more.

She looked away from the camera and glanced at Sean.

Oh god, she really had a type.

Moments later, the leopard thrust up from the edge of the riverbank and leaped into the herd, falling out of sight. He was a flash of shining fur and muscle, then he was gone.

Juni took a breath and sat up. "Lost him."

"You had him." Sean was beaming at her. "Damn, you had him, and I'm betting that footage is going to be amazing."

"I can't wait to download it and work on it. It's going to be dark, but I can lift it."

Their driver Luke turned the Range Rover and headed back to camp. Juni sat in the far back row of the vehicle, leaning on Sean's shoulder and looking at the frames he'd captured with his camera.

"These are by far the best pictures of a leopard I've ever gotten in Kenya."

"And at night."

"He's gorgeous, right?"

June nodded, but her eyes were already drooping. The adrenaline was starting to wear off, their night game drive was over, and they were leaving the next day. The drone of the engine, as they bounced along dirt roads, lulled her to sleep.

"This reminds me of home," she murmured. "Dry air. Dust."

"That smell after it rains."

"Yes." She felt him lean his head on the top of hers.

Sean had been dutifully sleeping in the twin bed like a schoolboy, despite Juni's protests, but that night she wanted him with her.

She knew sex was off the table. They weren't there yet. Or they were past it. Maybe they'd lost their chance forever. He'd be gone tomorrow, and she wanted him close.

"When was the last time you slept with someone?"

He froze. "Juni—"

"*Slept*." She kept her head on his shoulder and reached for his hand. "Not sex, not fooled around, slept."

He pulled back and looked at her with a slight frown marring his forehead. "I don't remember."

She pulled his shoulder back and laid her head on it. "You're sleeping in the big bed tonight. There's plenty of space. I know that twin isn't comfortable."

"I'm fi—"

"Don't say you're fine." She shook his arm. "Just shut up. We're both exhausted; we'll just sleep."

THEY SLEPT, but halfway through the night, Juni woke, and Sean was lying next to her, looking at her while she slept.

"Sorry." He blinked and turned away.

"Was I snoring?"

"No." He smiled. "The moon was coming through the screen" —he pointed overhead to the screened skylight in the canvas— "and it woke me up. You were there, and the moonlight was right on you." He lifted his finger and trailed it along her cheek. "It's hard to look away from you."

She didn't even have words. She pressed her head forward and kissed him. She knew it was against their unspoken rules. She knew he'd probably pull away.

She did it anyway.

To her endless surprise, he didn't pull away. His kiss was tender and exploring, more like a first kiss than their passionate explosion in Chiang Mai. He kissed her lips, then the arch of her cheekbone. His fingers danced lightly along the edge of her jaw.

Juni had never felt more treasured in her life.

They kissed for what felt like ages, then Sean pulled her into his chest, she rested her head against his heart, and they fell asleep with their arms and legs in a tangle.

WHEN JUNI WOKE UP, and Sean was gone, she wasn't surprised, but it still hurt. She put on her traveling clothes and walked to reception to grab breakfast and a few more pictures of the resort before she caught the lunchtime flight back to Nairobi.

"Miss Juni!" Benjamin came running to her. "Mister Sean had to leave on the early flight—"

Of course, he did.

"—but he left this message for you." He held out an envelope. "I hope everything has been pleasurable during your stay with us."

Juni stared at the envelope. "He left me a note?"

"Yes." He shoved it toward her. "Do you need—?"

"I'm good." She grabbed it from his hand. "I'm... uh, can I get some coffee? I'll just go to the library to read this."

"Of course!"

Juni walked to the extended, raised platform covered by open-sided tents and sat down in a chair near a broad shelf of books.

She opened the letter from Sean and was unsurprised that it wasn't a letter, but a short missive of barely seven words.

Email me your address in Chiang Mai. —Spider

six
lost in thailand

Chiang Mai, Thailand

HE STARED at the address on his phone, then at the bundle of flowers in his hand.

What was he doing?

It had been three months since he's seen Juni in Kenya, but it felt so much longer.

He'd boarded a flight to Chiang Mai after a long conversation with his cousin Marcus in Cambio Springs. Marcus was back in the Springs. Things were going well.

Life was actually looking up.

Like Sean, Marcus had been one of the few Quinns to make it out of the Springs and find some success. Unlike Sean, Marcus had a wife and kids, and he'd decided to go back and try to make things better with Sean's friend Alex and the rest of his clan.

His cousin had assured him that things were going well. Life was improving. There were jobs on the horizon, and his great-uncle was still hanging on.

"Live your life, man." Marcus had been the closest thing that Sean had to an older brother. "No one is going to judge you, cousin. If your heart isn't here, it's not here, and nothing in the world is going to make it that way."

"Marcus—"

"We want you to be happy. All of us do. Me, Josie, even the old man. We don't want you here unless you want to be here. Don't let the past rule your life."

He'd taken a deep breath and tried to believe it. Then he'd looked at Juni's address in Chiang Mai for the hundredth time, gone online, and booked a ticket.

The call to Marcus was two months ago, and now he stared at the flowers in his hand, the enormity of what he was planning to do falling on his shoulders.

What are you doing, Sean?

Why are you waiting?

Why are you here?

She's twenty-four.

Sean tried to remember who he'd been at twenty-four, but that young man was as distant as the town he'd run from. He remembered being hungry, restless, and angry. So angry.

He was still angry.

Sean stared at the red flowers in his hand, sitting on a bench in Three Kings' Square and listening to the mix of languages as the tourists and residents passed. A bike nearly clipped his foot. The sun got higher in the sky. It started falling.

What are you doing, Sean?

The flowers started to wilt.

✳ 133 ✳

Sean stood, stared in the direction of Juni's apartment, and started to walk.

You have to do this.

You have to try.

His phone buzzed in his pocket, and he took it out to see his friend Alex's name on the screen. Alex was in the Springs.

Alex was working with Marcus.

Sean's heart was racing when he hit the button to take the call. "What happened?"

JUNI WAS EDITING photos when she heard the knock on the door. She called out "Just a moment!" then she saved the file and stood from the low table she was sitting at near the balcony.

She walked to the door expecting one of her neighbors, but a little boy was there holding a bouquet of wilted red flowers and a card like the ones at the florist shop on the end of her street.

"Hello." She smiled. "Are you lost?"

The boy shoved the red flowers at her and ran down the stairs.

That was weird.

Juni took the card and saw Sean's writing on the envelope.

What the hell?

She looked at the flowers, then at the card. Was he here? In the city? She set the flowers to the side and tore open the card. She'd been waiting for months to hear from him after his cryptic note in Kenya.

The note was short, which was no shock.

Neither were the contents.

I can't. You know what I want, but I can't do that to you.
You deserve every good thing in the world, Juni.
I'm sorry.
—S

To say her heart broke would be to admit that she'd been holding out hope, and that was a hard thing to own. She knew he was damaged. She knew he wanted her anyway.

"Do you want me to go?
"Nope. So you should definitely go."

That was it. That was Sean. It always had been and probably...

Probably that was all it ever would be. Stolen moments in different countries and always running away.

"Just know that when things get hard, I run away. That's what I do. That's what I'm good at."

Juni crumbled up the card and threw it in the trash. Then she took the flowers to her downstairs neighbors and left them on their front steps. She wasn't a fool. Life hadn't given her what she wanted, but she didn't throw nice things away.

She didn't waste beauty when it was offered to her.

She walked down the street, taking in the sights and sounds of the city around her.

You are allowed to be sad for one day. She blinked back tears. *Then you have to move on.*

Juni took a deep breath and walked up Moon Muang Road, the afternoon breeze cooling the tears as they fell down her cheeks.

To read the rest of Juni and Sean's story,
preorder Dust Born, coming October 2023.

And turn the page for an exclusive preview from Chapter
One of **Dust Born: A Cambio Springs Mystery.**

preview: dust born

Cambio Springs, California

SEAN QUINN STARED at the shot of whiskey the bartender poured into his glass. It was shot number three. If he drank it, he'd definitely be looking for a ride home. Two, he could handle, especially as long as he'd been hiding out at The Cave, but three? Nope. He'd have to call someone, and calling someone in Cambio Springs meant calling family.

It wasn't as if the sleepy desert town had a lot of Uber drivers, though with the new resort opening, that might not be a bad idea. He'd have to talk to some of the younger members of the clan—well, those who'd kept their noses clean—and suggest it.

"Ugh." He groaned and banged his forehead on the arm folded on the bar.

Tracey, the bartender who'd been watching The Cave that night, patted his shoulder. "Family stuff?"

"Isn't it always?" His voice was rough, no doubt from the second shot of whiskey. He reached for the third. To hell with it. He'd call one of the kids to come pick him up. It wasn't as if younger Quinn family members weren't used to scraping their elders off the floor of drinking establishments.

Nice family you got there, Quinn.

Yep. It was great. He shoulda never come back.

Never ever...

Sean Quinn had never fit into the isolated town of shapeshifters in the middle of the Mojave Desert, and it was impossible to blend in when you lived in Cambio Springs. Everyone knew everyone. Half the town was related to each other, and people who married or moved in knew the score.

Everyone had their place.

The wolf and cat clans battled for political and financial dominance in Cambio Springs. They were the most visible citizens. Doctors, lawyers, business leaders, and teachers. They were proud and fiercely protective of their weird, eccentric little community. The small bird clan kept to themselves, the most likely members of the Springs to roam around the world, though they always returned. The bear clan, who owned The Cave, were the guardians of Cambio Springs, quiet, old-fashioned, and rock-steady.

And then there were the Quinns. Cold-blooded reptile shifters, Sean's clan was smart, but conniving. Charming trouble-makers who were loyal only to themselves, the snake clan consisted of a strange melange of reptile shifters spread over Cambio Springs and the outskirts. A few were reliable, but most fell victim to the family inclination to get what they wanted or needed by any means necessary, which included lying, cheating, gambling, and bullying.

And then there was Sean, who desperately wanted to just go along and blend in.

He was an observer by nature. He loved watching people. Watching nature. He spoke through his camera lens, hoping to connect with those who found beauty in unexpected places. And prior to the year before, he'd managed to do that pretty well, keeping in touch with his closest childhood friends while forging his own path and traveling the world.

And then... it had all turned to shit.

The one reliable Quinn cousin in his generation—his older cousin Marcus—moved back to take over the reins of his unruly family and promptly been murdered by an ignorant and vengeful human. That meant the only semi-reliable one left was Sean. So when the family called, he came.

That was the rule in Cambio Springs, whether you wanted it or not: if family called, you came. The clans may have squabbled amongst each other, but within each clan, loyalty was sacrosanct.

Fuck. His. Life.

A heavy hand fell on his shoulder and Sean turned to see Oliver Campbell, one of his oldest friends and the new leader of the bear clan.

"Hey, Ollie. What's up?"

"I heard you were here."

"Yep." Sean blinked to clear his gaze. "Do you know you sound like a tractor engine?"

Ollie barely cracked a smile, so a slight curve of his mouth meant he thought Sean was hilarious. "A tractor engine?"

"Yeah. All rumbly and shit." He rubbed his eyes. "Is Allie here?"

"Home with the kids." Ollie slid onto the barstool. "Tracey called me. Said you looked like you needed someone to talk to."

"Fuck." Sean sighed. "Yeah, probably. I've got three kids in the clan suspended from school right now because they thought shifting into rattlesnakes to scare the new kid in class was a hilarious rite of passage. And now my sister is giving me shit, saying that the boy who the kids shifted on was provoking the Quinn kids, calling them 'white trash' stuff like that. So I don't know how the hell to deal with any of that. Do you?"

"Huh." Ollie grunted. "There are three rattlesnake shifters in the same class? That seems like a lot."

It would be. Usually more lethal shifters were spread out unless there was some threat to the community.

"Not three in one class. Rattler wasn't their natural form."

A shifter's natural form was whatever they first shifted into when they hit puberty. It was what they transformed into on full moon nights. If would always be their most comfortable and easiest shift.

For most shifters, variations on their natural form were possible, but difficult. Ollie's wife Allie could shift from her natural fox form to a coyote if she tried really, really hard. His friend Jena could shift into any number of raptors from her natural hawk form, but it took skill and a lot of energy.

Bears? Well, bears were always bears.

But among the snake clan, multiple forms were common. Sean's natural form was a diamondback rattler, but he could shift into nearly any reptile he studied. He'd tried lizards and every scaly thing imaginable. Constrictors and pythons, horny toads and water dragons. He was notorious and famous in his clan for his abilities.

Only his sister Maggie came close.

Ollie asked, "So is Maggie right? Were the kids provoked?"

"Man, I don't know. Half the time with that crew I feel like I'm bailing water out of a sinking boat." Sean motioned for Tracey to pour another shot in his glass. "The old man did what he could to raise us, but most all of our parents were shit. It started turning around with the younger kids, but most anyone from about twenty-five to fifty is mostly a mess. And this shit at school isn't helping. The principal—"

"Cat," Ollie muttered.

"Exactly. She has no patience for the little shits, and I can't blame her." He downed the shot and heard himself start slurring. "And here I am trying to hold everything together and be a parent to a bunch of teenagers when I don't even have my own fucking life figured out."

Sean could never tell what was going on with Ollie. Marrying the love of his life had done nothing to soften him. He was still about as understanding as a brick wall.

"Maybe I should call Alex." Ollie started to stand up.

"No." Sean put his head in his hand. "I'm just... venting. I'll be fine." *I think.* "And... I should go home. I have a meeting at the high school in the morning, because apparently that is a thing I do now."

Because fuck his life.

"Need a ride?"

At least there was that. If Ollie drove him, Sean

wouldn't need to call any of the teenagers he was supposed to be setting a good example for.

"Dude," Sean said. "If you could give me a ride, that would be—"

"No need." Ollie hit his shoulder. "Check out who just came in. Destiny is on your side, Quinn."

Sean turned and blinked.

She wasn't destiny; she was disaster.

Juniper Hawkins was standing at the bar, holding a couple bags of what looked like takeout. She'd had blue streaks yesterday, but today they'd changed to gold and red. She walked toward the bar, her steps light and her smile wide. Her tan arms were slim and muscled from carrying around photography equipment, and her hair was pulled up into a messy bun.

She was so fucking cute he wanted to bite her.

"Sean Quinn, you still can't hold your liquor." Juni cocked her head at him, her smile never wavering. "Ollie, do I need to pour this one into bed?"

"If you could drop him at his place, you'd be doing me a favor."

"No." Sean pointed at her food. "You're heading home. To eat."

"It's fine," Juni said. "Jena and Caleb are gone, so I'm being the lazy auntie. I can drop you off. After all" —her smile turned from bright to mischievous— "we are neighbors now."

"YOU CAN TALK TO ME, you know." Juni glanced across the truck cab. "I don't bite."

But I do.

"I'm just trying to figure out why you're still here," Sean said. "The feature for the magazine was done months ago."

"And was very well-received. Rani suggested we work together on the next project. Want to go to Costa Rica?"

God yes. "I can't right now." He rubbed his eyes. "And seriously, if you're getting job offers in Costa Rica, why are you here?"

"Maybe I like this town."

Sean snorted. "Why on earth would you like this town?"

"My brother is happy here. He wasn't happy for a long time, you know? Our mom wasn't the nicest to him."

I know how that is. He leaned against the cool window of the pickup, pressing his forehead to the glass and closing his eyes to the oncoming headlights.

"I've got time," Juni said. "I've got a nice amount of cash tucked away. My apartment in Thailand isn't going anywhere, and I'm enjoying the dry air. There's really nothing else I'd rather do than hang with my brother and his new family, you know?"

"You never mentioned him before." Sean swung his head around to look at her. "Like... *before* before."

Juni's smile was impish. "So by *before* before, do you mean—?"

"You know what I mean."

"But do you mean India?" She batted her eyelashes innocently. "Or Thailand? Or did you mean Kenya, when

❋ 143 ❋

we were staying at that lodge and there was only one tent so we—"

"I'm not talking about... I mean, yes, *that* before, but we're not talking about Kenya. Or Thailand."

"Or all the times when you completely avoided any and all personal questions and told me" —she dropped her voice— "'Listen Juni, this isn't happening.' Only it happened anyway and you just felt really guilty about it."

His mouth was gaping. He knew it, he just couldn't control his mouth enough to close it.

Screw you, whiskey. This was all Ollie's fault. Somehow.

"I didn't sleep with you," he blurted out. Probably because of the not-controlling-his-own-mouth thing.

Her eyes flashed. "No, you did not. Didn't you want to?"

"You know I fucking did."

"We were both adults, Sean. So why—"

His laughter cut her off. "You were twenty-two, hippie girl. I was nine years older than you and we worked together."

"And now I'm twenty-five and you're thirty-four and we *don't* work together, so what's your baggage, Quinn?"

He closed his eyes and shook his head. "You have no idea."

"Fine, be secretive. Just don't give me shit about not spilling everything about *my* family, okay? You sit over there being the King of Avoidance and we both know it."

"Fine." Sean crossed his arms. "We both have our secrets." He had so many secrets, they threatened to break his back.

"That's right, we both do. And don't patronize me

again. I may be young, but I've been on my own since I was eighteen."

It was another thing they had in common, but Sean kept his mouth shut. His desire for Juni wasn't something he could indulge in. It wouldn't be fair to either of them. He'd once thought that maybe one day they would be able to make something work but...

Not anymore. Not with Marcus gone and Sean being tied to Cambio Springs. Juni may have been parked in his hometown for a few months, but she was not the type to settle down.

She turned off the main road and right after the Black Bird Cafe, Jena's diner. She went south and away from the main road, out to the edge of town where Caleb and Jena's house sat. They had a few acres stretching from the main road to a winding creek where cottonwood trees lined the banks.

Juni—in her apparent quest to drive Sean crazy—had taken the beautiful restored Airstream trailer behind Jena and Caleb's house as her own while she was back in the States and figuring out what to do.

Sean was living in the trailer on the far edge of Jena and Caleb's property near the creek. He was working on fixing it up in exchange for rent. He owned the title to two houses in town, one of which was massive, but his sister was living in that one with some of the other single Quinn girls, and another clan family that had just moved back to the Springs was living in the other. Since it was just him, Sean was camping out at Jena's.

It had nothing to do with being near Juni. At all.

Of course it does, you masochist.

Sean would have to be blind not to miss the laser-like eyes of Caleb Gilbert, Chief of Cambio Springs Police Department, new father and husband, and Juniper Hawkin's older half-brother. It was probably only Jena's intervention that had kept Caleb from murdering Sean already.

"So you know my baby sister, huh?"

Sean watched her from the corner of his eye.

Did he know Juni? Not as much as he wanted to.

Not nearly as much.

Dust Born is now available to preorder from Amazon!

about the author

ELIZABETH HUNTER is a ten-time *USA Today* and international best-selling author of romance, contemporary fantasy, and paranormal mystery. Based in Central California, she travels extensively to write fantasy fiction exploring world mythologies, history, and the universal bonds of love, friendship, and family. She has published over thirty works of fiction and sold over a million books worldwide. She is the author of the Glimmer Lake series, the Elemental Legacy series, the Irin Chronicles, the Cambio Springs Mysteries, and other works of fiction.

also by elizabeth hunter

Ink

Hooked

Grit

Sweet

Made in the USA
Columbia, SC
09 July 2023